'Pethidine, D

'OK,' Sophie sa
flinched at the so

'Very wise,' Reith said softly. 'I'll drop in
tomorrow to check on my handiwork; if it's
going to infect I should be able to tell by
then.'

'I can check it myself.'

'I check my own work.'

'So what do you charge for home visits?'

'You'll get my bill,' he said softly, and his
eyes locked on hers and held. 'I'll let you
know what you owe me. And maybe you're
right to be worried. . .'

Marion Lennox has had a variety of careers—medical receptionist, computer programmer and teacher. Married, with two young children, she now lives in rural Victoria, Australia. Her wish for an occupation which would allow her to remain at home with her children and her dog led her to begin writing, and she has now published a number of medical romances.

Recent titles by the same author:

A CHRISTMAS BLESSING
ENCHANTING SURGEON
DANGEROUS PHYSICIAN
DOCTOR'S HONOUR
PRACTICE MAKES MARRIAGE
STORM HAVEN
ONE CARING HEART

BUSH DOCTOR'S BRIDE

BY
MARION LENNOX

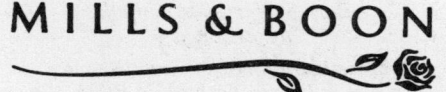

MILLS & BOON

Thank you to Charlie Franken and Dick Brumley, Department of Conservation and Natural Resources, for their generosity in sharing their specialist knowledge.

*MILLS & BOON, the Rose Device and
LOVE ON CALL are trademarks of the publisher.
Harlequin Mills & Boon Limited,
Eton House, 18-24 Paradise Road, Richmond, Surrey TW9 1SR*

© Marion Lennox 1996

ISBN 0 263 79534 9

*Set in Times 10 on 10½ pt. by
Rowland Phototypesetting Limited
Bury St Edmunds, Suffolk*

03-9604-49832

*Made and printed in Great Britain
Cover illustration by Kay Boyce*

CHAPTER ONE

IT WAS Dr Lynton's aim to photograph a koala—not to squash one.

Tyres squealed and gravel flew as Sophie Lynton hit the brakes. Her hired car slewed sideways. The car finally ceased its skid at a ninety-degree angle to the road, headlights beaming uselessly into the bush.

Had she hit it or not?

What was the creature doing sitting in the middle of the road on a blind bend anyway? Sophie's fingers gripped hard on the wheel and she closed her eyes, reacting to her fright. She'd spent hours searching tourist trails for koalas, found none and made herself late searching. The guest-house she'd arranged to stay at tonight didn't seem anywhere down this dirt track, it was dark, she was lost, and now. . .

Now somewhere under her car was a koala. Now she had to emerge from the car and look.

'Don't let it be dead!' With the silent plea echoing in her head, Sophie gingerly opened her car door and stepped out onto gravel.

The koala was straight in front of her headlights.

The huddled fur-ball didn't move as Sophie knelt over it. The koala was crouched less than a foot from the bumper bar, terror-filled eyes reflecting the lights from the car. Sophie's heart twisted in pity.

'Oh, you poppet! I've scared you even more than you scared me.'

The koala appeared unmarked, but it stayed motionless. Its eyes looked blank and stunned.

With the koala where it was, Sophie couldn't move the car. She'd have to shift the animal. How did one shift a koala?

Sophie ran a hand through her dishevelled curls and bit her lip. Having just completed two years in the casualty department of St Joseph's, handling emergencies was supposed to be Sophie's forte—but this was a smaller and fluffier emergency than she was used to.

The koala wasn't much larger than a toy—and it looked just as cuddly. Surely she could move it?

'OK, koala,' she said softly. 'You can't sit there all night waiting for my car or something else to squash you. I'll lift you off to the side of the road.' Decision made, Sophie grasped it firmly around its midriff from behind.

Mistake! The small creature slashed back with one savage swipe, slicing Sophie's arm from elbow to wrist.

Pain shot upward in an agonising lance. The koala was released as Sophie gazed at blood welling from a deep and jagged tear.

This wasn't in the tourist brochures. Sophie was in Australia, land of sun, wilderness and cuddly koalas. . . And dreadful roads, and obscure road maps and loneliness and stupid koalas who tore the arm trying to save them.

'I think. . .' Sophie said unsteadily to the darkness around her, 'I think I want to go home.'

Home. . .

London, England. Two thousand miles, or was it three. . .?

'Some honeymoon,' she whispered as blood from her injured arm dripped steadily down onto gravel. 'I'm not even married, and Kevin's still in England and I'm lost and you've cut my arm to the bone, you stupid koala, and I don't know how to shift you. If you keep sitting there I can't move my car without squashing you. . .'

It was too much. Sophie gave a desperate sniff and let an unaccustomed tear trickle down her cheek.

It was the first time Sophie Lynton had cried for years. Sophie scorned tears. Her mother cried to manipulate all around her, and Sophie had sworn never to follow her example. Here, though. . . Here there was only the koala, and the koala wasn't about to be manipulated by weeping.

She was wrong. There wasn't just the koala. As Sophie reached into the car for a towel to wrap her arm she caught the sound of an approaching vehicle. By the time she'd wrapped the gash, the sound was a rattling roar—some sort of vehicle was approaching with the sedateness and rattle of age.

It was just as well it was sedate. Sophie's car was blocking a blind bend and a fast car could have careered straight into hers. As it was, the approaching truck clattered round the corner, the driver slammed on the brakes and it came to a halt with ten feet to spare.

Sophie leaned back against her car. The pain from her arm was making her feel nauseous and the darkness and loneliness of the place was making her just plain scared. To be stuck in the dark in a strange country on a road that seemed in the middle of absolutely nowhere. . .

What she wanted was a capable middle-aged couple to emerge from the truck—people able to tell her she was safe, move the koala, direct her to her guest-house and maybe throw in some sympathy for good measure.

This was no middle-aged couple. It was a lone man, and at first sight he wasn't in the least reassuring.

Sophie's car was lighting the road, and the man emerging from the truck left his lights on as well. He stood by his ancient vehicle as he surveyed Sophie and koala, and Sophie felt the fear within her swell even more.

The man was filthy. He was in his thirties, large, lean and rugged. Tanned, muscled arms emerged from a sleeveless shirt, he wore faded jeans and battered leather boots, and a couple of days' stubble obscured his strongly boned face. Sophie couldn't see the man's eyes. Underneath the wide brim of an ancient hat they were hooded shadows.

Instinctively Sophie took a step back, frighteningly conscious of the isolation of this place—and the man's size.

'This isn't the most sensible place to park, lady.' The man's voice was deep and harsh. He clearly wasn't wasting time on pleasantries.

'The koala was on the road. . .' Sophie's response came out a nervous whisper and the man threw her a curious look before striding across to the front of her car. His easy, long-legged gait spoke of country rearing—a man at home in this setting.

'You hit it?'

'I. . .I don't think so.' Sophie flinched. Why wouldn't her voice work properly?

The stranger ignored her, kneeling down by the koala and slowly running his eyes over the frightened creature. Then, once again, his hooded eyes looked up at Sophie.

'You're a tourist?' His voice implied what he thought of the species.

'Y. . .yes.'

'Well, for once there's no damage.' He ran his gaze thoughtfully over the position of her car. 'Though you could have killed yourself as well as the koala. You'd be a damned fool to be travelling at speed on these roads at night.'

'I wasn't. . .' To Sophie's dismay there were tears in her voice. Drat the man. 'If. . .if I was travelling too fast I would have hit it. But I can't. . .I can't get the koala to move.'

'You could try turning your headlights off. How do you expect a wild animal to move when he's effectively blinded?' The man sighed, not expecting an answer from one so patently stupid; then with one fluid movement he effortlessly lifted the small grey and white furred creature. One strong hand grasped the scruff of the koala's neck, the other its rump, and he lifted and carried the koala out well before him to evade the slashing of terrified claws. As the man reached the grass verge with his furry burden the koala let his opinion of proceedings be known, emptying his bladder in a long, steady stream.

'I agree. Tourists!' Incredibly, the man's deep voice was laced with laughter.

Ignoring the koala's waterworks, the stranger lifted the little creature into a fork of a gum tree and then stood back and watched as the animal clawed its way to safety. Finally he turned back to Sophie.

'You can turn your car now,' the man said dismissively, clearly glad to be shot of her.

'Thank. . .thank you.'

Something in her voice reached him. The man pushed his hat back from his face to reveal a mass of dark hair, and his deep-set eyes narrowed.

'Is there something else wrong?'

'No. . .' Sophie turned and fumbled with the door of her car but the man was fast, covering the distance between them in three long strides. As her car door swung open his hand was reaching out to stop her. He grasped her injured arm through the towel and she gave an involuntary whimper of protest.

Her sound of pain made him release her. He drew back, but not far enough to let her climb into the car. He was so close. . .

'What the. . .?' He stared down at his hand and his square, work-soiled palm showed red with Sophie's blood. His eyes widened in understanding. 'You tried to lift the koala?'

'It scratched me.' Sophie attempted to shove her way into the car but his body blocked hers. He stood like immovable iron. 'Please. . .' she whispered. 'Just let me go. . .'

'That's some scratch.' Ignoring her protest, the man reached once more for her arm, holding her this time by her fingers and pulling back the towel to expose the wound.

For a long moment there was silence and then the stranger gave a soundless whistle. 'This is going to need stitching.'

'I know.' Sophie pulled her arm back but her effort was futile. 'I'll get it seen to when I get where I'm going.' The culmination of fear and shock was making her voice tremble.

'Look, I'm not planning to rape you, lady.' The harshness was back in the man's voice and the eyes staring down at Sophie were filled with self-mockery. 'This is nasty. I'll drive you back to my place and—'

'No!' There was no disguising the fear in Sophie's voice.

He sighed. Pulling off his hat, the man ran a hand through jet-black hair and his voice gentled. 'Lady, I'm the local doctor. Five minutes from here I've a surgery with all I need to stitch this arm.'

'A doctor!' Sophie's eyes widened in incredulity. 'You expect me to believe that?'

'Yeah.' The man's eyes met hers, and the self-mockery was again plain. 'Strange as it may seem, I do, and there's no other doctor within fifty miles of this place. Like it or not, you're going to have to trust me. Now, let's shift your car off the road and get you somewhere I can work.'

'No!' Sophie's voice again rose on a desperate sob of fear, and it checked the stranger.

There was a long silence while Sophie's breath came too fast into the silence. Finally the man lifted a hand to her shoulder and the touch made her flinch.

'Hey, I really am a doctor.'

The man's rough voice gentled still more, seductive

in its comfort, and it was close to Sophie's undoing. She was scared, she was dead tired and she was confused. How dared he make her want to weep still more. . .?

'I don't. . .I don't care,' she faltered. 'Please. . .I'm supposed to be at Mrs Sanderson's. She runs a guest-house and according to my map it's supposed to be near here. I've been looking, but the map's useless. It has roads where no roads exist. . .'

'Maybe it's because our roads aren't bitumen high-ways,' he suggested. 'You must have missed the sign. It's about half a mile back on the last turn-off.' The stranger's hand was still on her shoulder and his touch was doing strange things to Sophie's body. She badly wanted to sit down.

She swallowed desperately, pulling away from his hand. 'Then, if you don't mind. . . Will you let me go? Mrs Sanderson will organise me medical help when I get there.'

'You mean organise a nice clean doctor—maybe a nurse or two in white uniforms standing in attendance? Hey, how about a full-blown casualty department with the odd consultant surgeon?' The ironic laughter was back.

'Look, just stop playing games.' Sophie's voice shook with fear and pain. 'I appreciate your help, but Mrs Sanderson was expecting me hours ago.'

The man was silent. In the absolute stillness of the bush night they could hear the scratching made by Sophie's koala as it made its way up into the heights of its gum tree. There was nothing else.

He was too near. The man was less than a foot from Sophie, his body blocking her from her car. He was six inches taller than Sophie. If he wanted to hurt her. . .

He hadn't made a move to hurt her. Why was he so frightening?

It was because he was so darned male. He even

smelled male, Sophie acknowledged—the strong smell of a man who'd been doing hard physical labour for hours. Some doctor. . .

'You can't drive.' He was watching her face, and his voice was still gentle.

'I can,' she said defiantly. 'If you get out of my way I'll show you.'

'And if I don't. . .'

'Then. . . I'll. . .'

'Scream?' Once again that mocking smile, twisting the corners of his wide mouth. His teeth flashed white in the darkness. 'And our friend koala will dash down to the rescue. . .'

'Please. . .' There were the remains of tears in her voice and Sophie despised herself for it. He mustn't hear it.

It seemed he had. After an endless moment he finally stood aside.

'I guess, if I offered to drive you, you'd refuse?'

'Yes.' What did he expect? That she would get in that ramshackle vehicle with him. . .or he would drive her car. . .? He had to be kidding!

The wide mouth twisted again. Once more he reached for her hand, taking her fingers in his strong grasp.

'Is there any numbness?'

'No,' she snapped. 'I've checked. I haven't damaged the flexor tendon or nerve.'

'Oho. . .' His look of amusement deepened. 'So you'll play nurse to my doctor?'

'Don't be stupid.' She pulled back again and he released her arm. 'I know what I'm talking about. I can drive and I don't need your help.'

His dark eyebrows lifted. 'So gracious a maiden in distress! Give me koalas any day.' He shrugged. 'OK, lady. Turn back and take the left fork. Moira Sanderson's place is half a mile along on the left. You'll drive at no more than five miles an hour, and I'll be travelling straight behind. My place isn't much further on and I'm damned if I can reconcile my conscience with leaving you to faint through blood loss. If you so much as think about putting your foot on the accelerator I'll run you off the road, and if you feel dizzy then you stop and I'll drive you.'

Sophie stood back, slightly stunned and very confused. 'Th. . .thank you.'

'I don't want your thanks. In one sentence you infer I'm intending rape and in the next you thank me nicely. You're not making sense. So just move, lady. It seems I have work to do tonight, and the sooner we get on with it the better.'

On which enigmatic statement he wheeled abruptly away and climbed back into his truck. Without another word he started his engine, then idled the truck in neutral while he waited for Sophie to get in her car and do the same.

What on earth. . .?

Panic welled within her. She didn't know where on earth she was. He could be directing her anywhere. . .

'Stop it, Sophie,' she told herself on an hysterical sob. 'You're letting your imagination run riot.'

'Why did he say he was a doctor?' she then demanded of the darkness.

'Don't think about that. Maybe you misunderstood and he's done some first-aid course. You don't have a choice, Sophie, but to do what he says. Police stations and hospitals are hardly thick on the ground around here.'

She had no choice.

With a sob of disbelief at the mess she was in, Sophie finally climbed into her car. She steered her car back onto the road, and the stranger's truck moved into place behind her. Wherever she was going, the stranger was clearly following.

CHAPTER TWO

IT SEEMED the man's intentions were honourable.

The house was where he had said it was. Half a mile down the side-road was the sign she'd been looking for for two hours. SANDERSON'S GUEST-HOUSE. Sophie turned into the driveway with a gasp of relief.

And she was suddenly alone. Behind her, the truck's horn blared and it rattled on. Duty done, it seemed the stranger was leaving her to her own devices. He had no ill intentions after all.

The relief made her feel dizzy.

As the lights of the ancient truck disappeared into the distance Sophie felt the first twinge of conscience. She'd sounded dreadful—exactly the sort of tourist he so obviously thought she was. He'd helped her and she'd been so frightened that she'd been obnoxious. She was in a strange country—she'd expected the worst and she'd made her distrust obvious.

He hadn't helped, though. The man must be some sort of simpleton, telling her he was a doctor. . .trying to persuade her to go to his 'surgery'. . .

She couldn't think about it. Her arm was throbbing with a grinding ache and it was still sluggishly bleeding. She pulled to a halt and laid her weary head on the wheel in a gesture of pure relief to have finally arrived.

Despite her pain and confusion, the stranger's dark eyes still mocked her. The truck lights were gone, but the image of the man stayed with her.

It was fright that had left such an impression, she thought wearily. It had to be.

There were stirrings from within the guest-house. Lights were being flung on, and a middle-aged lady came hurrying down from the veranda.

14

'Dr Lynton. . . Oh, my dear, is that you? I've been so worried. You were supposed to be here hours ago.'

Sophie climbed wearily from the car and looked around her. This was the place she and Kevin had dreamed of—or rather she had dreamed of and Kevin had nodded and agreed and thought of something else.

The house looked just like the pictures in the brochures she had read back in London—a massive white weatherboard house with wide verandas and rambling roses growing in profusion everywhere, their heady scent mingling with the eucalyptus from the gums encircling the house. The mountains loomed behind, black and forbidding against the night sky, and the sound of running water near-by reminded Sophie of the clear streams and waterfalls to be explored in the morning.

'I nearly called the police.' Moira Sanderson's wispy bun bobbed back and forth in a gesture of decision. 'When you called and said you'd be coming alone instead of with a new husband—and then you didn't come at all. . .'

'You thought I might have driven off a cliff in a moment of suicidal madness.' Sophie gave a wry smile as she collected her suitcase from the luggage compartment. 'It's not that bad, Mrs Sanderson. Kevin's still coming and we still are getting married.'

'Any man who lets urgent business interfere with his marriage sounds a worry to me, dear,' Moira said roundly. 'Can I help with the suitcase?' Then she gave a horrified gasp as Sophie moved under the veranda lights. 'Oh, my dear. . . What on earth have you done to yourself?'

What indeed. . .?

She must look like something out of a horror movie, Sophie though ruefully. Her jeans and white blouse were liberally smeared with her blood. The car wasn't air-conditioned, so Sophie had driven with the window open to escape the heat—and her shoulder-length

chestnut curls were caked with dust from the dirt roads.
She still had the odd tear stain on her face, she guessed,
and she'd touched her face with her injured arm, leaving a streak of blood drying down the length of
her cheek.

Looking the way she did, it would hardly be surpris-
ing if Moira Sanderson ran inside and closed the door
in her face. The landlady, however, was made of
sterner stuff.

Moira Sanderson grasped Sophie's suitcase from her
in an instant and placed an arm around her waist.
'You look about to drop,' she said soundly. 'What
happened?'

'A. . . There was a koala on the road. . .'

'A koala.' Moira shook her head, needing, it
seemed, to know no more. 'Oh, dear. They look so
cute, but when they're frightened they certainly know
how to defend themselves.' She looked down at
Sophie's arm. 'And you tried to pick him up? They'll
do that every time.'

'I didn't know they scratched. . .'

'They're wild creatures, dear, despite their cuddly
appearance. Ugh. It'll infect too if that's from his
claws. There should be a sign on every tourist brochure
saying "The Health Department Warns Koalas Can
Be Injurious To Your Health". Like on the cigarette
packets. Well, I guess it's too late to warn you now.
A bath, something to eat and a doctor I think. . .'

A doctor. . .

It seemed, despite what the stranger had told her,
that there was a doctor in the valley. Moira Sanderson
was reassuring.

'Inyabarra's tiny. The town consists of one general
store, one pub and a consolidated school because our
children can't make that awful bus trip across the
mountains each day—but we do also have a doctor,'
she told Sophie proudly.

Sophie had been firmly ushered into a bath, and it had been all Sophie could do not to prevent the kindly landlady drying and dressing her herself. Now Sophie sat in the kitchen in Moira's all-enveloping dressing-gown, sipping hot sweet tea and trying to block out the pain in her arm. 'Dr Kenrick's been here for the last five years,' Moira continued, 'and where we'd be without him I don't know. He looked after my Patrick all through his last illness—and without him Patrick would have died in hospital fifty miles from the place he loved.' Moira sniffed. 'Enough. You don't want to hear my life story. I rang Dr Kenrick while you were in the bath. He'll be right over.'

'Maybe. . .maybe I can drive to him—if the surgery's not too far away.'

She didn't want to. Sophie's voice sounded doubtful even to her. If she was her own patient she wouldn't advise driving—and as for finding her way back into the tiny township and back again. . .

'No.' There was no thought of her trying, it seemed. Moira was shaking her head with decision. 'Dr Kenrick said he'd be right over—and if I'm not mistaken that'll be him now.'

There was certainly a vehicle approaching.

A vehicle. . .

Sophie sat bolt upright, her tea splashing onto the table before her. The sound was unmistakable. There couldn't be two such decrepit vehicles in the valley.

'Does. . .does Dr Kenrick drive a truck?' she managed. 'An old one. . .?'

'Yes, dear. We tease him that he should drive a Mercedes but he says on these roads he's better with something that's already been jolted to bits and has nowhere left to jolt.' The landlady had crossed to the kitchen door and was standing with it open, waiting for whoever was arriving to walk in out of the night.

Sophie took a deep breath, a silent prayer echoing in her head. Let it not be him. . .

Of course it was him. The man had transformed himself, but Sophie would have recognized her rescuer anywhere.

A shower, shave and clean clothes had turned the man into a possibility of a doctor, but it had done nothing to conceal the sheer, rugged maleness of the man. He was wearing clean trousers and a neat open-necked shirt, his strongly boned face was clean shaven and all Sophie could see were those mocking, deep-set eyes. . .

'Well, well,' he said, standing at the door and surveying the seated, dressing-gowned Sophie with a mocking smile. 'What have we here, then? A dose of flu?'

Sophie flushed crimson.

'Dr Kenrick, this is my guest, Sophie Lynton.' Moira Sanderson was looking a little confused. 'I thought I told you on the phone she'd had some trouble with a koala.'

Sophie stayed speechless. The man's eyebrows rose in mock astonishment.

'You don't say? They're getting more vicious all the time. There used to be a myth that koalas just eat eucalypts—but how many tourists were eaten last year, Moira?'

'Very funny,' Sophie whispered, shaking herself out of her daze. 'Are you. . .are you really a doctor?'

'Of course Dr Kenrick's a doctor!' Moira Sanderson was shocked.

'A real one, I mean?' Sophie was struggling through a fog of confusion.

'My degrees are on the wall at my surgery,' the man told her. 'As you'd have seen if you came to my surgery when I invited you.' He walked across and lifted her throbbing arm. 'I'm Dr Reith Kenrick, lady. M.B.,B.S. from Melbourne University. Graduated seven years ago, followed by two years internship and then country practice for the last five years. Satisfied?'

'But you looked so. . .so. . .'

'Dirty?' The wide mouth flashed in a grin. 'Maybe doctors are allowed to get dirty once in a while.'

'Dr Kenrick, Sophie's a doctor as well,' Sophie's landlady announced, clearly at a loss as to what was going on. 'She's come all the way from England.'

'A doctor. . .' Reith Kenrick was carefully examining Sophie's wound and hardly seemed interested. 'Doctor of what? Cartology?'

Cartology. . . The study of map-drawing. Sophie's breath drew in on an indignant hiss. 'Now who's being insulting?' she asked.

Reith nodded absently, his mind once again clearly on his work rather than her, and Sophie felt herself strangely at a loss. He saw her as a cut arm rather than a person—and she didn't like the sensation.

She looked up at him as he inspected her arm and her impression of distance deepened. It wasn't just that he was uninterested in her. Reith Kenrick seemed a person apart. Even as he'd smiled at Moira Sanderson in greeting, there had been something in his eyes that suggested a deep and constant reserve.

'Let's check the hand.'

'I told you,' Sophie managed, unnerved and totally out of her depth, 'there's no tendon or nerve damage.'

'I'm not intending to sew a cut I haven't checked—so co-operate or find yourself another doctor.' Reith Kenrick raised his mobile eyebrows again. 'Or stitch it yourself.'

It was her right arm. To stitch her own right arm. . .

She looked up into those dark, mocking eyes and felt a surge of helpless anger.

For heaven's sake. . . He was a doctor. He was here to help her and, like it or not, she needed help. Somehow she found the resources to summon a smile.

'I'm. . .I'm sorry.'

'Very good.' Once more he switched into professional, absent mode. He lifted her fingers. 'Tell me what you feel?' One after the other he tested sensation on each fingertip, examined her movement and finally nodded.

'You've been lucky.'

'It's my lucky day,' Sophie said through gritted teeth. 'My lucky week.'

'Dr Lynton's supposed to be here on her honeymoon,' Mrs Sanderson offered helpfully. 'But her fiancé had to stay behind in England.'

'Maybe he ran out of clean shirts,' Reith said drily. He turned toward his bag to fill a syringe with local anaesthetic, avoiding Sophie's glare of pure hatred. He turned back, his attention solely on her arm. 'This will sting a bit. Try and be brave.'

Sophie's fingers curled. She gritted her teeth, but not with pain. This man was impossible.

Her anger carried her nicely through the next few unpleasant moments. Reith Kenrick was a skilful operator. He cleaned the wound with meticulous care, and then sutured it closed with tiny, neat stitches.

'You'll have a hairline scar,' he told her as he tied off the last stitch. 'Unavoidable, I'm afraid.'

Sophie looked down at her stitched arm. It was a skilful piece of work. In fact, she had been lucky. There were many doctors who couldn't have done as neat a job as this.

With an effort she pushed her anger to the back of her mind. Sure, this man was unlike any colleague she had ever met—but he had helped her. He had not only rescued her from the roadside but he had come out on a house call to someone who had been blatantly rude to him.

'I really am grateful,' she said softly. 'Dr Kenrick, you've been very patient. . .'

He straightened from adjusting the dressing and looked down at her. Clean-shaven, tanned and immaculately dressed in well-tailored trousers and linen shirt, the man was impossibly handsome.

Impossibly. . . If Sophie hadn't been happily engaged to her Kevin. . .

What on earth was she thinking of? Sophie gave herself an angry mental shake.

'It's my job to be patient,' he said drily. His deep eyes mocked her, as though he guessed what she was thinking, and to her fury Sophie felt a tinge of colour surge across her face. 'So. . .if you're not into cartology, are you really a doctor of medicine?'

'I can't display my certificates on my surgery wall,' she told him, managing an apologetic smile with an effort. 'But I really am.'

'A general practitioner?' He was filling a syringe with antibiotic.

'I guess that's what you'd call me. I qualified three years ago and have been working in Accident and Emergency since then. Now—'

'Now you're supposed to be being married,' Moira broke in. 'Of all the inconsiderate males—'

'Kevin didn't mean to let me down.' Sophie shook her head, her fingers touching the stark white dressing on her arm. 'He's still coming. He's supposed to be here on Friday. This way. . .well, we'll just have the honeymoon before the wedding.'

'That's not how it was done in my day,' Moira said darkly. She peered down at Sophie. 'Eh, my dear, you look done in, doesn't she, Dr Kenrick?'

'She does.'

Sophie was struggling to rise but the effects of the night's events and loss of blood were taking their toll. Her legs felt unsteady under her, and her head spun sickeningly.

'I'll. . .I'll be OK. If I can just go to bed. . .'

'Her bedroom's the first at the top of the stairs, Dr Kenrick,' Moira said firmly, and there was no mistaking her message.

'No!'

'Yes.' Reith Kenrick's low growl was an order, and

Sophie was no match for it. She could hardly fight him off. He injected antibiotic with clinical efficiency, then, before she could try to rise, his arms came around to lift her to him. In an instant she was cradled against his hard, muscular chest.

'Put. . .put me down!' Her voice was hardly a squeak.

'I'll put you down in your bed.' Ignoring her protest, Reith was striding out of the kitchen toward the stairs. 'Put the kettle on, will you, Moira?' he called back to Sophie's landlady. 'I'll be down for a cup of tea after I dump this.'

This. . .

She really was an object. He saw her as a patient to be rid of as soon as possible. Reith strode up the stairs with long, easy strides and Sophie knew he might just as well be carrying a sack of potatoes. So. . .so there was no reason why her heart should be doing crazy backflips.

It was just that she was unused to being held by a man.

Kevin holds you, she told herself savagely, but the thought of Kevin was a dim, faint memory. All that was real was the warmth and hardness of this male body and the strength of his hands. . .

She looked up and found his eyes on her, his mouth twisting into a quizzical grin.

'Enjoying the sensation, Dr Lynton?'

'N-no!' It was an indignant gasp.

'Well, well. . .' His eyes mocked her as he pushed open her bedroom door with his foot. 'A cold lady. My sympathies to the absent Kevin.'

'I don't mind when it's Kevin—' Sophie bit her tongue in horror. What was she saying? She had no need to defend her relationship with her fiancé to this man.

'You don't mind if Kevin touches you?' His eyebrows rose. 'Lucky Kevin.'

Moira had pulled the bedding back on the double bed while Sophie was in the bath. Now Reith Kenrick lowered Sophie with exaggerated care and Sophie grabbed the sheet and hauled it up to her neck. Moira's huge dressing-gown was concealing but not concealing enough. What was it about this man that made her feel so exposed?

'Thank you,' she said stiffly. 'Now. . .now will you please go away?'

He didn't. Reith Kenrick stood looking down at her, his face a curious mixture of derision and pity.

'You're not having a very good time, are you, Dr Lynton?'

'Of course I am. I'm having a terrific time. I like coming on my honeymoon on my own. I like getting lost for hours on end in the middle of nowhere and being savaged by koalas. I especially like being laughed at by country doctors who haven't washed for days and who mock me and make me feel. . .' Her voice rose and to Sophie's horror she choked on an almost hysterical sob. She put her hand to her face in horrified dismay but Reith Kenrick was before her.

His long, lean fingers touched her face—lightly— in a feather touch of reassurance and comfort.

'You're exhausted,' he said softly. 'I'll give you something to let you sleep.'

'I don't want anything.'

'I'm sure you do. When the local anaesthetic wears off that arm will hurt, and there's nothing like a sleepless night in pain to make things worse.'

He moved swiftly from the bedside and out of the door, but in moments he was back, a syringe in his fingers.

'Pethidine, Dr Lynton? You know you need it.'

'OK,' she said ungraciously and then flinched at the sound of her voice. She looked up at the man standing before her, and found his eyes gentle with understanding. The desire to weep was almost overwhelming.

'Very wise,' he said softly and carefully inserted the needle. The tiny pinprick in her arm hardly hurt at all.

'I'll drop in tomorrow morning to check on my handiwork,' he told her.

'There's no need.'

'If it's going to infect I should be able to tell by then.'

'I can check it myself.'

'I check my own work.'

'So what do you charge for home visits?'

Oh, for heaven's sake. . . Why on earth had she said that? This man was bringing out the worst in her. Out on the roadside in the dark she had thought it was fear that was making her react as she was. Now here. . .

There was the same sense of fear, but it wasn't a fear of physical danger. It was fear of what her body was doing to her—of how she was reacting to this aloof, contemptuous colleague.

There was a long, long silence. For a moment Sophie thought he would wheel away from her bedside and leave her to her bad manners. Instead that mocking smile finally returned.

'You'll get my bill,' he said softly, and his eyes locked on hers and held. 'I'll let you know what you owe me. And maybe you're right to be worried. . .'

The drug Reith Kenrick gave her made Sophie sleep like a baby. She'd spent thirty-six hours travelling from England to Australia, and then another twelve in an unfamiliar car in a strange country, culminating in the koala incident. Now her body demanded its due, and it was past midday when she stirred.

The curtains were still closed but the windows behind them were open, and the soft linen folds were stirring gently in the warm breeze.

For a moment Sophie was confused and then the events of the previous two days came back in a distressing flood.

There was a pergola outside her bedroom window roofed with lush greenery and brilliant red flowers, the like of which Sophie had never seen before. The sun was dappling through as the curtains shifted with the breeze. Sophie lay back on her pillows and let the events of the past few days settle themselves from crazy kaleidoscope into some sort of pattern.

First there had been the telephone call from Kevin saying he was caught up in Belgium and wouldn't make it to their wedding.

Fine. It wasn't as though it was a grand occasion anyway. They'd booked the register office and let a couple of Sophie's best friends know—so it was a simple matter to cancel.

'Go on to Australia without me,' Kevin had laughed over the telephone. 'It seems a shame to waste a perfectly good honeymoon.'

'I'll wait for you.'

'Sweetheart, I don't know how long this will take. It could be days. It could be a week. If you leave tomorrow I'll try to be there by Friday.'

As he'd put the phone down Sophie had imagined she had heard the sound of a woman's voice in the background, softly laughing.

Kevin. . .

He was a high-flyer. He always would be, Sophie knew.

They'd been at university together—coupled at a time when Sophie desperately wanted to be a couple. She wanted to be a family more than anything else.

She didn't have a family of her own. Heaven knew where Sophie's father was—Sophie certainly didn't. Her mother was a cold, manipulative woman who moved from man to man with an eye for the main chance. There had never been anyone for Sophie— and what Kevin offered seemed too good to be true.

What did Kevin offer? Security. Admiration. A linking to someone—a sense of belonging. . .

She and Kevin had started going together when Sophie was seventeen—and that sense of belonging was so important that she couldn't end it.

But I will if he doesn't come on Friday, she told herself harshly, twisting the extravagant diamond on her third finger. Kevin. . .

Curiously, though, the desolation she was feeling wasn't for the man himself. It was for that sense of belonging that was so important to her. She'd be alone again. . .

'Completely alone,' she murmured. 'I was mad to come to Australia. Mad!'

There was the sound of voices below stairs and then a heavy tread, taking the polished stairs two at a time. A firm knock on the door. . .

'Y-yes.'

It wasn't Moira. She should know that step. It was as distinctive as the man's decrepit truck. Maybe it was his truck that had wakened her.

Reith Kenrick's head came around the door—and then his whole body.

'Well, well,' he smiled as he strode across to the bed. 'The lady's awake. Had enough beauty sleep, then, have we?'

'I told you I didn't need you to come,' Sophie said crossly, pulling herself into a sitting position and lifting her knees to her chin in a gesture of defence. Her sheet stayed tucked under her chin.

'Do people always follow your orders?' Reith asked politely. He crossed to the window and flung the curtains wide, letting the dappled sun pour into the room. 'Does Kevin?'

'That's none of your business.'

'No.' He grinned. 'I don't suppose it is.' He strode to the bed and perched beside her. 'Let's see your arm.'

She cast him a suspicious glare and thrust her arm out in front of her. To her disgust, he laughed.

'You'd like me to take your arm somewhere else

and inspect it?' he asked and raised his dark eyebrows at her.

Sophie took a deep breath, and suddenly found she was smiling back at him. Those eyes were compelling—and when they were filled with laughter. . .

'I'm sorry,' she told him, lowering her arm into his hands. 'I behaved. . . Yesterday I behaved. . .'

'Like a scared kid,' he smiled, and his eyes were warm with compassion. 'I know. Things got out of control. When did you arrive in Australia?'

'Yesterday morning.'

His brows snapped down. 'So you came straight from the airport here—and then got yourself lost? It's a six-hour drive from Tullamarine when you know the road.'

'I wanted to make the most of my holiday,' she said stiffly. How to confess she'd been hurt and confused by Kevin? and to stay still and think about it seemed the worst thing she could do.

'Mmm.' He was unwrapping her arm, and the sight of the wound reassured him. 'Great. No sign of infection. You've been lucky.'

'I. . . Maybe I have,' she said stiffly. An apology was certainly warranted and she had to make it in full. 'You. . .you've been really good to me and I didn't deserve it. If I were you I would have driven off and left me to my koala.'

That surprised him. The mobile eyebrows arched upward and his face stilled.

'I wouldn't do that.'

'No.' She met that look. 'I know you wouldn't.'

The sudden frisson of electricity between them shocked them both into silence. A butcher bird was cackling away to itself in the bottle brush somewhere in the garden, and the remaining silence seemed endless.

Reith rewrapped her arm in silence and then stood up.

'I have a suggestion,' he said at last, and his voice was hesitant.

'A suggestion?'

'About that account you owe.'

Sophie licked her suddenly dry lips. She looked down at her bandaged arm. Now what?

'Just. . .just tell me what I owe.'

'A day's work.'

'A day's. . .' Sophie shook her head. 'I don't understand.'

Reith shrugged. 'Easy. I need a doctor for a day.' He spread his wide hands. 'Sophie, have you heard of Chlamydia?'

The use of her first name disturbed her. She struggled to concentrate on the question. 'Chlamydia?' Sophie frowned. 'Yes. It affects the eyes—or there's a strain that's a venereal disease. . .'

'Yeah. Well, there's also a strain that's present in koalas.'

'Koalas. You mean. . .you mean the koalas here?'

'Mmm.' Reith ran a hand through his hair in a gesture Sophie was starting to recognise. 'Chlamydia's latent in the breed, but overcrowding brings it out. The animals here have multiplied vastly since we turned the district into national park and rid ourselves of the koala's predators—like domestic dogs.'

'So what does Chlamydia do to koalas?' Despite her discomfort in the situation, Sophie found she was interested. She was also interested in the way Reith's voice became deeper and his eyes darkened as he forgot her presence and talked of something he was interested in.

'They have the same symptoms as humans. It affects their eyes, and in extreme cases it causes blindness. It makes the animal listless and apathetic. Their coat becomes matted and dull, and generally loses condition. Sometimes their weakness kills them, but mostly the worst thing it does is makes the animal sterile.'

'And. . .and it's curable?'

'Yes. Remove the overcrowding and with a good diet the koalas pick up like magic—but the sterility is irreversible.'

'I see.' Sophie's knees were still tucked up under her chin but, unnoticed, her sheet had slipped so that she was only covered by her soft cotton nightdress. It no longer seemed to matter. 'What do you want me to do, then?'

'Get yourself rested first.' Reith grinned and Sophie managed a return smile. 'But today's Monday and you're here until at least Friday without your append-age fiancé.'

Your appendage fiancé. . . Sophie gave a soft chuckle, thinking how much Kevin would hate the description. That was how Kevin thought of Sophie, though. . .An appendage, to be discarded at will. . .

'S-so?' Her smile had slipped but Reith didn't seem to notice.

'The conservation and wildlife boys are having a drive to get as many koalas as they can out of the district in the next few weeks. They're shifting them to an area north of here where the koala population was decimated by bushfire a few years back. By next month, one of the main sources of koalas' food—the manna gum—starts giving off a toxin and the koalas have to change to alternative eucalyptus. The over-crowding problem becomes worse by a hundredfold.'

'So?'

'So I'm good with koalas. I act as the local vet when need arises, and I know how to handle them. It's too hot to transport animals today and tomorrow but we'll be working again on Wednesday, and we want to get a couple of hundred moved by the end of the week.'

'In case you hadn't noticed,' Sophie said mildly. 'I'm

not all that dab a hand at catching koalas and putting them in boxes.'

'No.' Reith's wide mouth twisted into a grin and Sophie found herself responding to the humour in the depths of his dark eyes. 'I am, though. I spent most of yesterday in the bush and I want to be back there on Wednesday.'

'And?'

'And I wondered. . .' He shrugged. 'I run a quiet medical practice. I'm on call as needed, basically, but I found yesterday it didn't work. I was raised in the bush and I'm better than most at scaling eucalypts and bringing koalas down—much better than some of the conservation guys—but while I'm up in the heights they're busy falling out of trees and they want me on the ground where I can minister to their broken bones and bruised egos. So. . .'

'So you'd like me to help?'

'I only help with their koala collection in the mornings mid-week, but I'm finding even that hard without medical help. And it's a great way to see all the koalas you'll ever want to see.'

Sophie gave a rueful smile. 'I've seen one koala and I'm starting to think that's enough.'

'You mean you won't help?'

Sophie took a deep breath. She looked up into those dark eyes, and for a moment was silent.

The eyes stayed watchful. This man was an enigma—an unknown. He was expecting her to refuse. She could see it in the set look of his mouth. He was expecting. . .

Nothing. The impression caught and stayed as her view of him shifted imperceptibly.

This man expected nothing of anyone. He was a loner. The gauntness of his finely boned face deepened her impression of solitude. Of solitude and rejection. . .

This man had been hurt somewhere along the way,

Sophie thought suddenly—and badly hurt at that. He expected nothing of anyone. He expected her to be a selfish little brat—and something deep inside her cried out to reverse that impression. She felt an almost overwhelming need to reach out and touch the forbidding face.

'Of course I'll help,' she said softly and watched the expression in his eyes change to wary surprise.

He collected himself in the same instant.

'Great. I'll collect you at six.'

'Six. . .' Sophie squeaked her dismay. 'Six in the morning, you mean?'

'Six in the morning.' He grinned. 'We work until ten and then call it quits. What do they say, Dr Lynton? "Mad dogs and Englishmen go out in the mid-day sun. . ." You might brave the heat to climb gum trees, Union Jack waving from your pith helmet, but koalas and yours truly have more sense. Medical emergencies permitting, we sleep in the shade.'

'Very sensible,' Sophie snapped and Reith grinned.

'That's us colonials for you. Always take the easy option and let you colonisers take the hard course.' He touched her face lightly with his finger and the touch set a tremor through Sophie's body that he must almost have been able to see. 'Will I see you on Wednesday, Dr Lynton?'

'I—'

'Great.' One more brush of those long, strong fingers and a heart-wrenching twist of the mouth. 'Goodbye until then, Dr Lynton. Take care.'

CHAPTER THREE

THE next day and a half passed in a lazy blur. Sophie slept, took gentle walks along the stream running behind the house, swam in the waterhole and generally let her exhausted mind slip into neutral.

It was too hard to think. . .

Neutral? Who was she kidding? It was too hard not to think of Reith Kenrick. . .

Kevin and the unknown woman laughing behind him on the telephone were somehow much easier to banish from her thoughts. As Sophie lay on the lawns under the canopy of eucalyptus, the pages of the book before her kept reflecting Reith Kenrick's shadowed face. Over and over. . .

On Tuesday evening as she sat on the veranda and helped Moira shell peas for dinner Sophie's tongue finally revealed her almost overwhelming curiosity.

'Moira, will you tell me about Reith Kenrick?'

She had meant not to ask. Her mouth came out with the request all by itself. She could have bitten her dratted tongue right off.

Moira was smiling.

'I wondered how long it would take you to ask.'

'It's just. . .I mean, with him being a doctor. . .'

'Curiosity's natural,' Moira beamed. 'And healthy too, I'd say. Your dratted Kevin. . .'

'Kevin couldn't help being delayed,' Sophie said firmly, but Moira just shook her head and kept podding peas. She'd demurred at Sophie's offer of assistance, but, as Sophie was the only guest, the two were fast becoming friends.

'Reith Kenrick's a loner,' Moira told her, peas shooting into her basin with speed, and Sophie nodded.

32

'I can see that.'

'Yeah, well, life's given him some kicks.'

Silence. Having asked the initial question Sophie couldn't ask more. She wasn't supposed to be interested in the man.

'I've known him since he was a baby,' Moira said finally. She was talking to her peas, her mind obviously wandering from Sophie—wandering back thirty-odd years to when Reith Kenrick was a child. 'Reith's mother and I were much the same age. We married at the same time, but she wouldn't have a thing to do with me. She thought she was too good for this valley—and maybe she was at that.'

'So why did she come here?'

Moira shrugged. 'Reith's dad was an artist—a good one—and he lived in the bush not far from here. I personally think his paintings are appalling—all tortured skeletons and staring eyes. Nightmare stuff. He made a mint, though, and was critically acclaimed throughout the world. Heidi was a model—and I wouldn't mind betting Heidi wasn't her true name, but she never let us call her different. She married Reith's dad in a blaze of publicity. Married for money and position, folks said, but a fat lot of good it did her. Reith's dad hated people. He lived a hermit's existence, and he abused alcohol and pills. . . He was violent too. Heaven knows the real reason Heidi married him—but she did and then found she was pregnant. In those days it wasn't easy to end a pregnancy—or you can bet Reith wouldn't be alive now. He sure as heck wasn't wanted.'

'But. . .they stayed married?'

Moira shrugged. 'I don't think Heidi's career as a model was exactly lucrative—and Reith's dad made a fortune. She'd leave every now again but flitted back when she ran out of money. Reith was left alone with the old man—and he was old. Nearly seventy when Reith was born.'

'And he looked after Reith?'

Moira snorted. 'If you can call it that. He put a roof over the boy's head. There was money for food and if Reith disturbed his father he was beaten. I know Social Welfare took Reith away for a bit—but the old man had pride and contacts in high places, so managed to get him back. Reith ran wild in the bush—growing more and more into himself. Then, in his teens, he suddenly got a bee in his bonnet that he'd be a doctor. He started going to school regularly and worked himself to the bone. His mum had disappeared completely by this stage—married an actor, I hear—and the old man died just as Reith qualified for medical school. Reith left and we thought we'd seen the end of him.'

'But he came back?'

'How could a boy used to a life of complete solitude become accustomed to the city? He said it drove him crazy. Reith Kenrick needs no one. He's learned not to need, and he's at home only in the bush. Now no one comes near him emotionally and he likes it that way. He's modernised his father's farmlet, turned it into a surgery, and it makes him enough to live on— though he inherited a fortune from his father's art. He doesn't need to work, but we hope he always will because he's a blessing for this place. Inyabarra's too isolated to attract either doctor or vet—and Reith Kenrick acts as both. We pray he'll never leave— though it condemns him forever to his hermit life. It seems, though, that that's what he wants.'

Maybe.

Sophie thought about that gaunt, hungry face and wasn't sure. An unloved child. . . A man who wore cynicism like a second skin. . .

She thought back to her own childhood, and her heart reached out to him. They had hoed the same lonely row—and maybe Reith had reaped the more bitter harvest. Sophie hadn't been ill-treated as a child.

She had just been ignored, and she knew how soul-destroying that could be.

Reith collected her right on six the next morning. Despite her protests, Moira had risen and given Sophie breakfast, preparing a vast morning tea for her while Sophie tackled coffee and toast.

'I'll never eat all that,' Sophie had protested but Moira had shaken her head.

'It's not just for you, dear. Reith will bring nothing—see if I'm right. If you know how much I've longed to get a good feed into that man. . . This way you can say you have too much and offer to share.'

Sophie grinned. 'He just might suspect your motives. I can hardly be expected to eat four rounds of salad sandwiches and a whole chocolate cake. . .'

She walked out to Reith's truck as it rattled into the yard, absurdly self-conscious in the cool morning light. It felt almost a betrayal of Kevin to be going.

For heaven's sake. . . Kevin was in Belgium with a woman she didn't know and didn't want to know. What possible harm was there in doing as Reith Kenrick suggested?

'Planning on staying a week?'

Reith climbed from his truck and took Sophie's basket from her. He was dressed again in his disreputable clothes, and, although he was now clean, the same frisson of electricity quivered through Sophie. Why did he make her feel like this?

'Pardon?'

He held up the basket. 'Provisions for an army.'

'Moira's organising.' She smiled, her heart doing silly jumps in her chest. She lifted her shoulders. 'My landlady seems to think you need feeding up and sees this as a glorious opportunity.'

He grinned, swung the basket into the truck and then held the passenger door open.

'I'll try to oblige. Ready for work, Dr Lynton?'

'I'm ready,' Sophie said steadily and didn't feel ready at all.

They didn't travel far. Two miles from Moira's house, Reith brought the truck to a halt in a clearing a little off the road, on the banks of the same creek that ran through the Sanderson guest-house grounds.

There were already people there, most in khaki uniform indicating wildlife officers, with a few civilians interspersed.

'Like me, they're the ones who can climb trees,' Reith grinned. 'And who know enough of koalas not to trap animals already severely affected by Chlamydia.'

He introduced Sophie briefly and she was greeted with easy friendliness.

'Another doctor? What'd you do to get another medico here, Reith?' they demanded. 'Kidnap her?'

'Can we keep her?' one of the officers asked and they all laughed. Sophie's slim figure in her tight jeans and soft blouse brought general approval.

'There's a fiancé coming on Friday,' Reith growled drily. 'Hands off, boys.'

'So what's he doing letting you come out to the Antipodes on your own, Doc?' the same officer grinned at Sophie. His eyes were warm with admiration. In this predominantly male group she was causing a considerable stir. 'He must have a few kangaroos loose in his top paddock, I'd reckon, letting you come this far on your own.'

They left her laughing, a trace of unease running behind Sophie's smile. What *was* Kevin doing?

The men started efficiently preparing the individual cages, with little time for pleasantries. There was work to be done, and they wanted it done as fast as possible.

'If we get our quota done this morning then we won't be driving late tonight for release,' the man in charge told Sophie as they worked. He looked a question at Reith. 'We can call on Dr Lynton for any medical problem?' His doubt was clear. Sophie hardly looked a competent medical practitioner in her denim. Sophie drew in her breath in an indignant gasp.

'I know you'd like a nice antiseptic doctor in a white coat,' she managed. 'But I dressed according to what I perceived local custom required.' She cast a meaningful glance at Reith. 'And at least I don't stand in need of a shave.'

Her crack brought a shout of laughter from the men, and Reith was subjected to good-natured teasing as they scattered into the trees. He took it in good part, Sophie noticed, but there was still that aloof air about him—he held himself back.

Sufficient unto himself. He had to be. He'd learned the hard way.

To begin with she had little to do. She sat on a fallen log by the creek and watched the men near to her work.

The technique was simple enough. The men raised long, extendable poles into the trees, a red flag on the end. This flag they positioned over the koala's head. Frightened, the koala moved downward, the red flag inexorably following, driving it still further toward the ground.

It worked fine until the man on the ground became more of a threat than the red flag, but that was usually not until the koala was fifteen or twenty feet above ground. Then the koala headed out on the nearest branch and stayed there.

That was the end of the easy part. The final capture was effected by the hunter climbing the tree, positioning himself in a fork and working with another pole. This pole had a noose on the end. The noose slipped over the koala's head and tightened as it was released from the pole. Then the animal was jerked back from its hold on the branch and lowered fast to a waiting captor on the ground.

Simple! Except there was no way she was going to try it, Sophie thought, mindful of those dreadful claws.

These men made it look easy—and it wasn't the least bit easy.

Her first patient appeared after half an hour. The man had loosened his hold a fraction of a second too early as he placed a koala in its cage—and was savagely scratched for his efforts. Reith's bag was well-equipped for such a wound and twenty minutes later the man's wound was cleaned, dressed and he was back in a tree.

'Most scratches don't need stitching,' Reith had told Sophie. 'These guys know what they're handling—and when they see those claws coming back at them they take evasive action.'

Nevertheless there were two gashes that did require stitching and Sophie could see what Reith meant when he said he hadn't been able to help with the koalas when he was needed medically. If he'd had to clean up every time he needed to inspect a cut, he'd get nothing done.

As it was, Reith moved with twice the speed of the other men, capturing koalas with an ease the conservation officers could only envy. They used him too to check animals they were unsure could withstand the move. If there was the least doubt, Reith did a fast examination when he brought his own koala back to the group of cages.

'We should have a veterinary officer on site,' the man in charge told Sophie. 'But there's another group of us ten miles south and the vet's there. Doc Kenrick's every bit as competent—or more so—at telling us whether a koala is fit or not. He seems to have some sort of sixth sense. . .'

A sixth sense. She wouldn't doubt it. Reith Kenrick seemed almost fey. He worked swiftly and silently, and the more Sophie watched him the more intrigued she became. Wilderness doctor. . .

A blaring horn made her turn toward the road, breaking her train of thought. She'd been left alone for the moment, the men working further and further from base as the koalas nearest the clearing were captured.

A family sedan, coated with dust from the gravel road, was pulling fast into the clearing, and the driver's hand was hard on the horn. Instinctively Sophie stood and hurried toward it, sensing the same urgency in the way she'd seen people arrive at Casualty.

'Dr Kenrick! Please. . .I need Dr Kenrick. . .' A woman in her early twenties, her face stained with dust and tears and eyes huge with fright, tumbled from the car. She was staring wildly round the clearing and there was only Sophie in view. 'Is he here? Oh, for God's sake, is he here?'

The woman made to run straight past Sophie but Sophie's hands came out to catch and hold her.

'Reith Kenrick's in the bush. I'm a doctor. How can I help you?'

'A doctor?' The girl cast Sophie a wild, disbelieving look and then stared frantically past her, willing Reith to appear. 'Dear God. . .'

'What's wrong?' Sophie raised her voice to a curt, authoritative command, the voice she had perfected in the years she had spent trying to calm hysterical relatives.

The girl's long blonde hair was falling over her eyes. She pushed it away, swiping at her tears. 'My. . . my baby.'

'He's in the car?'

'She. . . I. . . Oh, God, I don't know what to do.'

Sophie released her and moved the ten steps to the car with lightning speed. A fast glance through the rear window and she was hauling open the door, and lifting a baby from a capsule in the back seat.

The infant—a little one of maybe four or five months—was limp in Sophie's grasp and it didn't take a medical degree to know what was wrong. Sophie put a hand on the child's face and flinched at the feel of fever. The child's temperature must be forty-two or

-three—and she was still swaddled in blankets.

Almost in the same movement she had used to lift the child Sophie hauled the blankets away, sinking to crouch in the dust so she could rest the child on her knees.

'What. . .what are you doing? Are you really a doctor? Oh, why doesn't Dr Kenrick come?' The girl stared hopelessly down at her child.

'I'm really a doctor,' Sophie snapped. 'How long has she been fitting?'

'Fitting?'

'How long has she been limp like this?'

'About. . .maybe about fifteen minutes or a bit more. She's got a cold but Dr Kenrick told me she didn't need antibiotics. This morning her cold seemed a bit better but I was feeding her and she just sort of rolled her eyes back in her head and went stiff. Then. . .I don't know. . .I thought she was dying and I shook her—and she went all limp.'

'How hard did you shake her?' Sophie demanded, her heart sinking. Shaking on its own could cause a cerebral bleed in a little one this age.

'Not. . .not hard. Just a couple of gentle shakes. Then. . .I knew Doc Kenrick was working out here, so I just wrapped her in her blankets and drove like fury. Oh, God, do you think she's dying?'

Sophie didn't answer. Her mind was racing and she had no time to find words of comfort.

The baby had been convulsing for fifteen minutes. The blankets were off the child now, but how on earth to get her cool fast? Instead of cooling the feverish child, the woman had heated her still further, wrapping her in blankets and placing her in a sun-drenched car. After fifteen minutes of continuous fitting there was a major risk of brain damage. They had to get her cool.

There was only one fast way.

'Come with me,' Sophie ordered and ran, not looking behind to see if the young mother followed.

The girl did.

A hundred yards away the creek bed dropped steeply away from the level ground. It was a four-foot drop to the water, with sheer, sandy sides. Sophie stared down at the sluggishly moving stream. How deep?

There was only one way to tell. She handed the child back to her mother and slid, feet first, down into the water.

The water hit her body in a chilling shock, cool and clear from the mountains above, and no more than waist-deep. Sophie steadied, then hauled herself up on the narrow bank, and held her hands up for the baby.

'Give her to me,' she demanded. 'Fast.'

'What. . .what are you going to do?' Fear was still trembling through the woman's voice. Clearly she thought she was dealing with a mad woman—and she wasn't about to hand her precious baby over.

Sophie took a deep breath, willing her voice to be calm and for her to sound as if she knew what she was doing.

'Your baby is fitting because she's running a temperature and has overheated,' she told the woman. 'This is the only way to get her temperature down fast.'

'But—'

'Give her to me,' Sophie demanded harshly. She was balancing precariously just out of the water. 'I know what I'm doing. You have to believe me.'

The girl cast a wild look round, still willing Reith to appear, but there was no one—only this mad, English-accented girl standing knee-deep in water and demanding her baby. She cast a scared look down at her child's lifeless face, and reluctantly handed down the baby. Two seconds later Sophie had slid back into the water and was lowering the baby slowly down against her chest.

This was less than ideal. In a hospital setting, Sophie would undress the baby and bathe her gently in water slightly less than skin temperature. The next alternative was to wash the child down with wet towels—but here, where there was no ledge on which to stand and work beside the water, to waste time undressing the child and trying to get wet cloths up and down the bank was to court disaster. After fifteen minutes there could still be permanent damage anyway. She just had to hope that the shock of immersion into cool water could be tolerated without further damage.

The limpness ended almost immediately. Sophie felt the baby's tiny body tense as the water soaked through her clothes. Good grief. . . The baby was dressed in a little woollen dress, with singlet underneath, by the look of it, and tightly buttoned matinée jacket. There were buttons and ribbons everywhere. It would have taken five precious minutes to undress her. Cute little woollen booties were on her feet and a little knitted cap was on her head. Adorable—but totally impractical in today's heat, and with blankets as well. . .

They'd shrink now, Sophie thought grimly, and the baby would be better off for its ruined clothes. Summer heat was hardly layette territory. Even if the child was well, she should be wearing little more than a nappy.

'OK, sweetheart. . .' The layers of wool were letting the cold seep in gradually, giving some buffer from the shock of cold on hot skin, but by now the clothes were thoroughly wet. Sophie managed to flick off the useless bonnet from the little one's head and lowered her so the back of her neck and head were in the water.

'Come on, little one,' she murmured, watching the rolling eyes. 'Come back to us.'

On the bank above, the young mother stared down with desperate hope. She had to trust Sophie, but Sophie could see in the way she stared down that she thought she was crazy to do so.

'Is she. . .?'

'Give her time,' Sophie said, softly splashing water onto the little face. 'It'll take time to get her core temperature down—'

'I want Dr Kenrick!' It was a heartfelt wail, and as if in answer to the plea Reith was suddenly on the bank, staring down at Sophie and baby.

'Dr Kenrick. . .' The young woman grabbed him as if she were clutching a lifeline. 'Stephanie. . .she's gone all funny and this woman says she's a doctor and she's going to drown her. . .'

Reith put her gently aside. In one lithe movement he swung himself over the embankment and slid down into the water beside Sophie.

'What seems to be the trouble, Dr Lynton?'

Sophie ignored him. Her eyes were only on Stephanie. Was she imagining it?

She wasn't. The focusless eyes were changing, fixing, staring up at Sophie with shock. Sophie felt the shift in the way the baby lay in her arms. Stephanie was back in charge of her body, and she writhed in indignation and fear.

Another tiny wriggle, and then the rosebud mouth dropped open. The child's eyes narrowed, and she let out a feeble wail.

It was one of the sweetest sounds Sophie had heard. She looked up at Reith and her eyes laughed with sheer joy.

'She's back with us.'

'So I see.' Reith looked down at the child in Sophie's arms. 'After fairly drastic treatment, wouldn't you say?'

Sophie flushed crimson, her delight in the child's recovery somewhat abating. Then she looked down at the angry little furrow on the baby's brow and the intelligence glaring up at her and her delight returned. There seemed little possibility of brain damage here.

'I dare say there's diazepam in your car that I could have searched for and injected her with to stop the convulsion, Dr Kenrick—or a bucket somewhere I could use to fetch water to wash her down with,' she said softly. She was trying to unbutton the baby's matinée jacket as she spoke and Reith moved to help her. To hold a writhing baby and undress her at the same time was no easy task. 'But it would have taken time, Dr Kenrick, and I figured after fifteen minutes of convulsions what we didn't have was time. What would you have done in the circumstances?'

Her voice held a trace of defiance. Reith cast a swift glance up at her and then concentrated again on the fiddly buttons. His long, surgeon fingers unfastened them much more swiftly than Sophie's could.

'I would have done exactly what you did, Dr Lynton,' he said at last. 'Well done.'

The crimson flush didn't fade one bit. Small praise for a simple procedure, but it was enough to make the cool of the water she was standing in fade to insignificance. Sophie warmed from the inside out.

The warmth grew. Reith concentrated on the buttons. It was crazily intimate, to be standing waist-deep in water with the baby between them. Their fingers touched as the baby's clothes slipped away and the strange feeling Reith engendered in Sophie took a stronger hold. He was so darned competent. . . He was so darned male!

Finally the baby was undressed, only her sodden nappy remaining. By now her crying had become a furious frenzy, small fists pummelling uselessly in the air.

'No damage at all, it seems.' Reith smiled, his hands reaching out to steady Sophie as she pushed herself through the water toward the bank. Where his hands touched her, the warmth was heat.

Men had appeared above them on the creek bank, drawn by the unaccustomed sound of a baby's cry. Reith took Stephanie firmly from Sophie and handed the baby up to waiting arms.

'Jenny, I'd sit down under the gum trees and feed her,' Reith told the anxious young mum. 'She won't settle until she's on the breast, and she'll make herself hot again screaming.'

'I'll just dress her again first,' the young mother started as Reith hauled himself up the bank and turned to pull Sophie after him.

'No.' Sophie and Reith spoke in unison and Reith grinned.

'It seems we have medical unity,' he told the small group of onlookers, steadying Sophie on her feet and casting a quick, concerned glance down at her arm. Traces of blood were showing through the drenched dressing. He touched it lightly, looked a query up at Sophie and she shook her head. She was fine.

Reith nodded, accepting her need for him not to fuss. He crossed to where the young mother stood. Jenny's face was ashen and the hands holding her dripping baby were shaking.

'Jenny, it's heat that made Stephanie convulse,' he told her gently. 'I know you're proud of Stephanie's beautiful clothes but you just can't use them except on cool days. Feed her in her wet nappy and leave her in that until she needs a fresh nappy—and then leave her in nothing more than a singlet and nappy until the temperature drops under seventy degrees. That's an order, Jenny.'

Jenny looked up at him, her face uncertain and unhappy. 'That's what you said yesterday, but my mum-in-law says you're wrong. She says you should have given her antibiotics and she says you have to keep her warm if she's got a cold. . . .'

There was silence among the group of onlookers. The men shifted uneasily, aware that Reith was being challenged, and Sophie stood silent. A first-time mother, and a very young one at that, had all sorts of pressures on her, and it was hard to withstand the pressures of a dominant mother-in-law.

'Do you think I'm wrong, Jenny?' Reith asked, his dark eyes fixing the frightened girl. His tone was gentle, as if he understood her conflict.

'N-no. Not now.'

'Would it help if I talked to your mother-in-law?' Reith asked and the girl's face cleared like magic.

'Could you? I mean. . .I know you're busy, but you see, Mum Lee knitted the clothes. She's been at me and at me for not using them and she was coming for lunch today, so I had to use them. And I've six full woollen layettes she knitted that Stephanie won't fit into by winter. . .'

She ended on a hiccup of a sob to match Stephanie's, and Reith smiled.

'Hey, Jen, settle down and feed Stephanie. I'll talk to your mum-in-law. Stephanie's her first grandchild but there are three more daughters and daughters-in-law to produce little layette-wearers. I'll settle her. I promise.' He turned to the men. 'Drama's over, boys. We've only fifty more koalas to go and we can call it quits for the day. Reckon we can make it?'

There were murmurs of agreement and the men moved off. Sophie expected Reith to go too but he came purposefully back over to her.

'Let's check your arm, Dr Lynton. It looks as if you might have broken your stitches.'

'I can check it myself,' she told him. 'Your koalas need you.'

'You need me first,' he told her firmly. 'I don't intend to let that arm get infected. It seems to me, Dr Lynton, that you could be very useful to me. You're one tourist worth looking after.'

Sophie stared up at him, her tongue for once bewilderingly at a loss. There was no reason at all for the warmth to build and spread over such a simple accolade. No reason at all. . .

An hour later the koala collection was complete. Sophie hadn't been needed again and, as Reith had needed to retie a couple of torn stitches, she was grateful to rest. She'd sat under the gums watching Jenny feed her baby, noting in satisfaction how the child drifted into sound, healthy sleep after the feed.

'You'd think she'd be cold in a wet nappy here in the shade,' Jenny said wonderingly, and Sophie shook her head.

'She's suffering from an infection that's putting her temperature up. By keeping her cool you're giving her body a better chance to fight the infection.'

Jenny cast her a shy look. 'You. . .you really are a doctor?'

'I am,' Sophie smiled. 'Trained in England, so I guess I'm not quite up to the standard of you colonials, but I'm a real doctor none the less.'

Jenny didn't return her smile. She clearly had something important on her mind.

'Would you. . .would you have given Stephanie antibiotics?' she asked. 'My mum-in-law will say that's why she had a convulsion. She says I should have demanded them yesterday when I took Stephanie to Dr Kenrick for her cold. She'll say now that Dr Kenrick was negligent not to give them.'

'Was there anything wrong other than a simple cold?' Sophie asked.

Jenny shook her head. 'No. Just a runny nose and a fever for the last couple of days.'

'Then I definitely wouldn't have given her antibiotics,' Sophie said firmly. 'A cold in the head is a virus, and antibiotic doesn't cure or even help a virus. If the virus causes an infection—for instance an infected ear—then there are bacteria the antibiotic can fight. Otherwise antibiotics are worse than useless.'

'Worse. . .'

'If you give antibiotic for every trivial illness then there's the chance that if Stephanie suffers a major infection the antibiotic will be less efficient. That's why Dr Kenrick wouldn't give it to her when you asked.'

'That's. . .that's what Dr Kenrick said.'

'Then your second opinion backs him up all the way,' Sophie smiled.

'How very supportive.' The deep voice behind Sophie made her jump six inches.

Sophie hadn't heard Reith approach. The man moved with the stealth of a cat. He smiled easily down at Jenny and her baby and his wide, easy smile encompassed Sophie and made her catch her breath. 'Satisfied, Jenny?'

'I. . . Yes. . .it's just. . .I didn't mean to doubt you. It's just that my mum-in-law made me feel like a bad mother for following your advice.'

'It's hard to know who to believe.' Reith nodded, his eyes gentle with understanding. 'But you're intelligent, Jenny. You need to trust your intelligence. Listen to what people say, make up your own mind—and then have the strength to stick to your guns.'

'I'll try.' Jenny smiled shyly. 'But you will. . .you will speak to Mum Lee this time. . .'

'I'll speak to your mum-in-law,' Reith promised. 'You said she was coming to your place for lunch?'

'Yes. . .' Jenny gasped, looking down at her watch, and then sighed in relief. 'It's only eleven. . .'

'I'll drop in at your place this afternoon,' Reith promised as Jenny rose with the sleeping baby. He raised his eyebrows at Sophie. 'In fact we might visit Mrs Lee with a deputation. Dr Lynton supports me nicely, don't you think, Jenny? We'll come together.'

'But. . .' Sophie shook her head '. . .I'm not—'

'Having lunch with me?' Reith lifted his mobile brows. 'It's too late for morning tea, and you try keeping Mrs Sanderson's chocolate cake to yourself, Dr Lynton, and I'll get in my truck and drive off with the lot. Now, we have all the koalas we need for the duration. I intend to take you back to Mrs Sanderson, make you respectable for home visiting and then take you and your basket of food with me on my rounds. I'll show you what country medicine is all about.'

'Make me respectable?' Sophie frowned and then looked down at herself. As she did she gasped. The water had made her blouse almost transparent. She wasn't wearing a bra, and as it had dried the soft fabric had clung to her nipples, moulding their shape. Sophie drew in an indignant breath and folded her arms across her breasts.

'Too late, wouldn't you say?' Reith grinned. 'I think it's very fetching but I doubt Jenny's mum-in-law will approve. So. . .let's make you decent.'

'You can leave me at Mrs Sanderson's,' Sophie said stiffly. 'If you don't need me again today. . .'

'Oh, I need you.' Reith smiled. 'Chocolate cake excluded, I'm beginning to think you have all sorts of possibilities.'

CHAPTER FOUR

ANY illusions Sophie had that Reith Kenrick was taking pleasure in her company were dashed well before lunch. Her desirability, it seemed, was purely medical.

'I jumped at the chance to introduce to you Margaret Lee,' he confessed as they left Mrs Sanderson's. Sophie was demurely dressed in a loose cotton frock and decent bra. She'd done the front opening up to the highest button on her throat—a stupid gesture, she acknowledged as she climbed back into the awful truck, since Reith didn't seem to notice. He didn't seem to notice her as anything more than a tool.

'Margaret Lee. . . Jenny's mother-in-law?'

'Yes.' Reith drummed his long fingers on the steering wheel, staring straight out at the dusty track. Sophie had the feeling, though, that he was seeing more than the dirt road. 'She's behaving as if she hates me.'

'I can't imagine why,' Sophie tried drily and Reith's dark eyes creased in appreciation.

'Yeah, well, strange as it may seem, Dr Lynton, the lady has been a faithful patient for the last few years. Now, though. . .I haven't seen her medically for six months and as far as I know she's not using anyone else but she's sending hate vibes all around the community. I don't know how many of the locals she's badmouthed me to—and I can't figure out why.'

'And you want me to find out?'

'That's the idea.'

'So why is Mrs Lee more likely to tell me than she is to tell you?' Sophie asked dubiously.

'Because you're a woman.'

'It doesn't endow me with any magical powers.'

Reith's mouth twisted in a half-grin. 'No. I guess not. But if I can leave you alone together maybe she'll give you a run-down on me—and just maybe she'll tell you enough to figure out what's going on.'

'She's ruining your practice?' Sophie asked caustically and Reith's eyes darkened in surprise.

'I don't know whether you're taking much of the local situation in, Dr Lynton, but the people here are stuck with me. If they have the time and ability to get themselves to the city to see an alternative then good luck to them. I don't worry about losing patients.'

'Then why. . .?'

'Why worry about Margaret Lee? Because I have a gut feeling she's running scared. Jenny and her husband are worrying about her. They say she's grumpy and withdrawn, and she seems to be losing weight. See what you think, Dr Lynton. I look forward to your professional opinion.'

Jenny Lee lived on the outskirts of the tiny town of Inyabarra, high on a ridge with a view of the town and mountains beyond.

'Jenny's husband's the local schoolteacher,' Reith told Sophie as they climbed the steps to the front door. 'Another Inyabarra boy who couldn't bear to leave the place forever.'

'I can understand why,' Sophie said softly, looking out over the spectacular view as they waited for Jenny to answer the door. 'This place is fantastic.'

'That's what all the tourists say.'

'And you don't believe it?' she threw at him and Reith shrugged.

'It's home.'

Before he could say more the door swung open, to reveal a shy, smiling Jenny. She was clearly nervous.

'Jenny? Who is it?' A querulous voice sounded from inside and Jenny grimaced.

'It's Dr Kenrick, Mum,' she called back to her mother-in-law. And Dr. . .'

Reith's hand caught Jenny's, stopping her short with the last word only half uttered.

'Not "Doctor",' he whispered urgently. 'Unless you've already told her what Sophie does, introduce her as Sophie.'

'But why not?' Jenny talked back in a half-whisper, her eyes puzzled.

'Because your mum doesn't like doctors at the moment and I want her to like Sophie.'

His smile of encouragement brought a conspiratorial gleam to Jenny's eyes. She grinned and led them through to the sitting-room.

Mrs Lee rose to meet them. She was a short, wiry woman, lean to the point of emaciation, with sharp, piercing eyes that missed nothing.

'I don't know why the heck you're here,' she said bluntly to Reith after casting an uninterested glance at Sophie. 'You've done enough damage already.'

'Meaning?' Reith surveyed the hostile woman with lazy interest, as though the last thing he would do was become offended by her words.

'I told Jenny to get penicillin for the baby's cold. You refused to give it to her. You'll kill my only grandchild. . .'

'Stephanie didn't need penicillin,' Reith said.

'Then why did she convulse?'

'Because she was overheated,' Reith said bluntly. 'Mrs Lee, I've told Jenny that Stephanie is not to wear anything more than a nappy and singlet from now on, until the temperature drops at least ten degrees. That's an absolute medical imperative and if she disobeys she'll be risking her baby's life. If you persuade her to go against my advice then it's you that's putting Stephanie's life at risk.'

'I won't do it, Mum,' Jenny said softly. 'I'm sorry. But I think Dr Kenrick's right.'

Mrs Lee's mouth twisted in a narrow line of disgust. 'You doctors. You don't know anything.' She cast a look of abhorrence at Reith and Sophie flinched. What had happened to make her hate him so?

Fear him so. . .

The thought flew into Sophie's mind so swiftly that she was sure she was right. This hate. . . She had seen it before when she'd had to tell a relative that someone they loved was dying. It was a way of rejecting truth— to hate the bearer of such tidings.

Reith had turned to the crib at the other side of the room where Stephanie lay in untroubled sleep. She was only in her nappy. Reith touched her forehead and gave a grunt of satisfaction.

'She'll do, Jenny. Ring me if you have any trouble but I doubt if you will now.'

'Thank you,' Jenny said gratefully. She looked over at the lunch table and then doubtfully at her mother-in-law. 'I don't suppose you'd like to stay for lunch?' she asked Reith and Sophie.

Reith shook his head and glanced at his watch. 'We've lunch with us, thanks, Jenny. We'll have it on the road.' He grimaced across at Sophie and lowered his voice, speaking to Jenny and her mother-in-law in a tone that Sophie could just hear but wasn't certain she was meant to. 'This dratted woman expects to be shown all the tourist sights—as if I haven't better things to do!'

Sophie cast Reith a look of astonishment and then looked quickly away at the message in his eyes. He was firmly telling her to shut up and play along. OK. . .

'Well, I haven't much time here. . .' Sophie said, and made her voice sound a little sulky. She wasn't sure what was going on but she wouldn't interfere with his game plan.

'Where are you from, dear?' Mrs Lee asked with interest and her look said it all. Anyone Reith didn't like was OK with her.

'England, of course,' Reith said in a bored drawl. 'Where else do you get that plum-in-the-mouth accent? And she's a dratted royalist. . .'

'There's nothing wrong with our royal family,' Mrs Lee said stoutly. She cast Reith a look of venom—as if she suspected him of being anarchist to the core—and then beamed her very nicest smile at Sophie. 'I'm English too,' she told Sophie. 'I came out here as a tourist, met my husband and stayed forever. But what. . .?' Another darkling look at Reith. 'What on earth are you doing with Dr Kenrick?'

Jenny was silent. She knew why Sophie was with Reith but Reith's eyes were telling her messages too and she was a smart young woman.

'Dr Kenrick's one of only two people I know around here,' Sophie said slowly. 'Yourselves excepted now, of course. I'm staying at the Sanderson guest house until my fiancé arrives. . .'

'Well, you must come to lunch with me,' Mrs Lee told her firmly. 'Tomorrow? I can show you my scrapbooks of the royal family—and if you're lucky there's sometimes a koala in my backyard.'

'So. . .why exactly am I going to Mrs Lee's for lunch?' Sophie asked cautiously as Reith ushered her once more into the truck.

'Because I'm worried about her, her family's worried about her and she won't let me near. You're the sacrificial lamb. Go in and ask questions, don't take no for an answer and find out what's going on.'

'Act as a nosy, rude tourist, you mean?'

'If that's the only way. You've nothing to lose. Margaret Lee cooks a great roast dinner.'

'Roast dinner! In this heat?'

'Yep,' Reith grinned. 'Speaking of dinner. . .'

They ate lunch back at Reith's surgery. His place was on the same meandering creek that ran through Moira Sanderson's, but higher on the ridge. The creek fell away below the house over a series of rocky falls, tumbling to the bush-filled valley below.

It was the perfect place for an artist, Sophie thought as she settled herself under the gums and stared appreciatively out at the view. Hardly an ideal place for a doctor's surgery, though.

'You look disapproving.' Reith emerged from the house, a blanket and wine glasses in his hands. He spread the rug and looked speculatively at Mrs Sanderson's basket. 'I'll provide wine.'

'Wine in the middle of a working day?' Sophie said in astonishment, and Reith grinned.

'One glass of wine and then a sleep, lady. Very civilised.'

'But if you get called—'

'One glass of wine isn't going to make any difference to my capacity to treat.'

Most unprofessional. Sophie gave a small, disapproving sniff and caught Reith's eyes gleaming laughter. Dratted man! She unpacked the salad rolls as Reith produced ice-cold moselle and poured. 'So. . . so when do you run clinic? You do run a clinic, I presume?' This was the most unusual medical practice she had ever encountered.

'Sure do. I run it in the evenings at this time of year. Clinic from five to nine, unless something crops up. It pays in a place like this to be flexible. The bush telegraph works pretty well if I'm called out and people understand. Next week it might be them who fall out of a tree and need all my attention when I should be running clinic. Most people around here are grateful that there's any sort of medical service at all.'

'And in emergencies? If anyone needs an anaesthetic—or you have more than one urgent case at a time?'

Reith shrugged. 'We cope. Anaesthetic cases get taken thirty miles to the nearest hospital—though

there's been the odd time I've acted surgeon anaesthe-
tist in one.'

'You're kidding!'

'I had a lady last year—a city hippy with ideas that
she'd like her baby born in the bush. She and her
partner took a tent high up in the hills behind Mount
Ranree and sat down to commune with nature until
junior appeared. Unfortunately undiagnosed pre-
eclampsia turned to full-scale eclampsia. She hadn't
been near a doctor for her pregnancy. By the time her
partner hiked down here to call for help and we got
men and four-wheel-drives up there she was too far
gone to move. Somehow we managed the most unanti-
septic Caesarian on record—and ended up with two
live patients. Bloody miracle!'

Sophie closed her eyes. The stuff nightmares were
made of!

'You didn't try to settle her first. . .' With eclampsia,
drugs could often settle the mother, giving time to
transport her to hospital.

'Whatever was happening was affecting the baby.
The foetal distress was marked. I had to make an
impossible decision. As it happened. . .well, she's suffered severe renal failure. There'll never be another
baby—so maybe my choice was the right one.'

'As you say. . .an impossible decision,' Sophie said
grimly.

'Something you don't get to face in inner-city
London.' Reith lifted a salad sandwich. 'Here's to city
practice and my escape from it. I wish you joy of it,
Dr Lynton.'

'You didn't like it?'

'I hated it.' His face closed.

'Too many people.'

'As you say.'

They ate the rest of their meal in silence. It was an
odd sort of silence, Sophie thought. Her mind was full
of questions she was aching to ask, and yet there was

a reserve about him that prevented intrusion. It was
a reserve that demanded respect.

The silence drifted on. The midday heat had become
a soporific blanket, casting a deep laziness over them.
Sophie's eyes drooped downward. She pulled her head
up with a jerk and found Reith smiling at her. Rather
than unsettling her, it only deepened her sense
of peace.

Of belonging. As if she was growing into the place.

Weird, total falsehood. How could she possibly
think that?

'Go to sleep,' Reith said gently, taking her shoulders
between his hands and pressing her toward the waiting
blanket.

'I'm not going to sleep with. . .' she murmured
and then her eyes widened as she heard what she
had said.

'Not going to sleep with me?' Reith smiled, a gleam
of laughter in the depths of his eyes. 'Very prudent,
Dr Lynton. What would the absent Kevin think of
that?' He released her and stretched out fully on the
blanket beside her, his disreputable Akubra falling
forward to shade his face. 'But sleep by me, Dr
Lynton? That's a very sensible thing to do. In fact,
until I choose to drive you home, it seems the only
thing to do—in the circumstances.'

To her amazement, Sophie slept. She'd never done
such a thing since childhood. It seemed the height of
indulgence—to sleep in the midday sun—and yet here,
with this man, it felt entirely natural. It was a deep
sleep that was the most untroubled she had had since
arriving.

Since. . .

Since when? Not for years had she woken like this, to
languorous contentment, as if the world had somehow
righted itself on its tilting axis and the way ahead was
different. . .

It wasn't different at all. Nothing had changed. She

blinked twice and then looked up as a shadow fell over her face.

'Lemonade, ma'am?' Reith Kenrick was holding two glasses filled with pale yellow, clinking ice cubes and sprigs of mint. 'Homemade.'

She struggled to a sitting position. 'What. . .what time is it?'

'Four o'clock. I've been out and done two house calls but it seemed a shame to wake you.' He grinned. 'You make a nice garden ornament.'

'Better than a concrete gnome.' Sophie smiled, accepting his proffered drink with gratitude. She looked up at him, suddenly shy. 'Th—thank you.'

He stood looking down at her for a long moment, his face shadowed. 'No trouble,' he said at last. He glanced at his watch. 'I'd better run you back to Mrs Sanderson's now, though. My clinic starts in an hour.'

'Could I. . .could I see your clinic first?' For some reason Sophie felt reluctant to leave. There was little reason for her to see this man again. On Friday Kevin would be here and then. . .

Friday seemed suddenly inexplicably bleak. She wasn't even sure if Kevin would come. That must be why the shiver of desolation crept through her.

'Sure.' Reith put his hand down to help her to her feet. His hand in hers made the shiver of desolation turn to something else.

For heavens' sake, Sophie Lynton. . . What on earth are you thinking of?

She was thinking of this lean, solitary man smiling down at her with a smile that committed nothing— that said he was pleasant and courteous and that was all. He wanted nothing. Totally self-sufficient. . .

Why did that trouble her so much? Reith Kenrick was nothing to her. Or was he?

He was looking down at her, his dark eyes creasing in swift concern.

'Is something wrong?'

She gave herself a swift mental shake and withdrew her hand from his grasp. 'No. Nothing, thank you.' She gave him her brightest smile and bent to lift the rug she'd been sleeping on. 'Lead on. . .'

He showed her through the clinic with the same detached courtesy and noncommittal friendliness she was learning to expect. He expected neither interest nor praise in his beautifully set-up little surgery, and his eyebrows rose in a cynical question as she gave it.

'You've seen better set-up surgeries than this in London.'

'Yes, I have,' Sophie agreed. 'And I've also seen worse ones. What I haven't seen is such a well-equipped situation for one doctor.' His tiny theatre was set up with the latest technical equipment. It glittered with clinical cleanliness, and Sophie blinked at the situations he was obviously prepared for. 'Surely it's not cost efficient?'

'To have equipment such as X-ray machines for one doctor?' Reith queried and shook his head. 'No, it's not cost efficient. Try telling that to the next farmer who comes in here with a broken arm and neither the time nor the money to go to the city for treatment.'

'The farmers round here aren't prosperous?' Sophie queried.

'You could say that,' Reith said drily. 'We get a lot of alternative lifestylers who come to me as a last resort and can pay very little—and there are the few who are struggling to keep old family farms going. The land round here's been marginal for farming for years. The farmers used crown land for grazing, but now the place is national park the cattle can't be grazed on government land and it's sending a lot of our people to the wall.'

Our people. . .

Did Reith think of the locals as his people?

'Why did you come back here?' she asked softly. 'Was it the place—or the people?'

'The place,' he said bluntly. 'I don't need people.'

'No one?' It was such a blank statement that Sophie was startled.

'I don't think anyone does. Where does involvement with people get you, Dr Lynton? Where does attachment to the absent Kevin get you?'

'It just might get me a family and children and warmth and laughter. . .'

'Or a whole heap of heartache.'

'That's cynical.'

'Honest.'

'So what about Mrs Sanderson?' Sophie said stoutly. 'She and Patrick had thirty years. . .'

'And then?'

'He died,' Sophie agreed. 'But surely those thirty years were worth something?'

Reith shrugged. Not to him, they weren't, his shrug said, and he looked at his watch. 'How the hell can I judge? I just know that I'm not buying into emotional baggage. I'll show you my father's studio if you like, then I'll have to take you home.'

A dismissal. She had earned as much from probing. Emotional baggage. . . Sophie bit her lip as she crossed through the door Reith was holding open.

The room he led her into took her breath away.

It was all window, with an almost circular view of the forest outside. The creek swept downward over rocks just outside the window and the huge plate glass swept upward so high that Sophie felt her eyes being drawn to the mountains in the distance.

It was no longer being used as a studio. Easels were still set up but they held finished paintings—and good ones at that.

This was a room Reith lived in, it seemed. There was a massive settee, its ancient leather upholstery softened and splitting with age, a vast Persian rug over the floor and books scattered in low bookshelves along the edge of the huge windows.

Sophie drew in her breath. She had never been in such a place. A swift glance behind at Reith and she wasn't all that sure that he wanted her to be here. His face was closed and empty. He was a courteous host showing a darned nuisance of a tourist the sights before getting rid of her.

She wouldn't be hurried. She couldn't. He had shown her this place of his own free will and she was going to look. He hadn't been compelled to show her.

She walked slowly from painting to painting. Many were the tortured abstracts Mrs Sanderson had described—all skeleton and harsh, tortured lines—but there were others. . .soft water-colours whose brilliance screamed out from the easel and whose contents reflected a pain she was starting to know. Like father, like son. . .

There was one. . .

Sophie stood before a small water-colour and looked at it for a long, long time. It was a bush scene, a mirror-still lake with a woman's face reflected through the trees. The face was superimposed on the scene as though part of it and yet apart—as if the woman was staring down, asking questions of her reflection. The woman looked out through the trees as if the forest were the bars of a cage.

There was something familiar about the woman's face. Sophie glanced back to Reith. The same fine bone structure. . . The same. . .

What?

The same closed look. This woman too had shut herself off. The forest was closing in on her and she wanted no part of it. Its beauty was all around her and yet she was closing it out, allowing it not to touch her even though she was part of it. The eyes were brooding and aloof as though she was planning—yearning to escape. There was a bleakness about her, though, that said escape was impossible.

A tiny label across the bottom said *Bush Bride*.

'Your mother?' Sophie said tentatively and Reith nodded. 'She didn't like the bush?'

'My father never should have brought her here. It's no place for a woman.'

'There are women here who are happy.'

'If they're born here maybe.'

'So if you marry—'

'I won't marry.' Reith's eyes flashed ice and Sophie grimaced. She was really stepping where angels feared to tread here. And yet. . . The solitude in this man's eyes was almost pain, and Sophie had never been one to ignore pain.

'Because your parents might have been unhappy is no reason—'

'Do you mind?' he snapped. 'What do you think this is, Dr Lynton? A counselling session? I don't ask your advice. If you want to sort out a marriage try concentrating on your own. Your nice, convenient boyfriend who's going to supply you with family and children. . .'

'Kevin's not convenient.'

'No. He's twelve thousand miles away. And you're hardly breaking your heart over him, now, are you?'

'That's none of your—'

'Business,' he finished for her. 'Now who's talking? But that's all marriage is, isn't it, Dr Lynton? Business. A nice, convenient hot-water bottle. Security for your old age.'

'Kevin's not. . .'

'Not what? Like other men? That's nonsense, Dr Lynton, and you know it. This love business. . .'

'Love business. . .' Sophie was wallowing way out of her depths. She didn't understand what on earth was going on to cause the bitter barbs being flung at her. She was caught in a conversation she wanted no part of, and yet she couldn't stop.

'Do you seriously think there's a one and only love in the world?' Reith demanded. 'If Kevin didn't arrive on Friday, would you break your heart? Oh, your pride would be hurt, and your plans for the future, but what else?'

'That's implying I'm marrying for convenience.'

'Aren't you? Doesn't everyone?'

'No!' It was a cry of anguish, no small part of which was caused by the seed of doubt that he could be right. She couldn't think that. She loved Kevin. Kevin was all she had. . .

'How much do you love your Kevin? Certainly not enough to prevent you reacting to me when I carried you to bed the other night.'

'I didn't react to you.'

He shook his head. 'Liar.'

'You arrogant toad.' The colour drained from Sophie's face and she faced him square. Her breath was coming in short, harsh gasps and her eyes flashed fury. 'You don't have the faintest idea. If you think for one moment I'm attracted to you. . .'

'Oh, not personally,' he agreed, watching her with an interest one might bestow on a rather interesting specimen in a jar. 'On any attractive male who comes into your orbit. Because Kevin isn't exclusive, is he, Sophie? He's just the one whose bank balance, lifestyle and ego match yours—'

'No!'

'It's true,' he went on relentlessly. 'You don't love him exclusively or your body wouldn't betray you. Exclusive love doesn't exist.'

'It does!' It had to. Sophie sounded like a desperate child. Who was this man to be throwing these ideas at her—to be attacking her? Who was he?

'Prove it,' he said softly, dangerously, and before she could move he had crossed to where she stood. Her arms were swept behind her, gripped like a vice, and his dark head lowered to hers. While one hand held her wrists with effortless ease, the other raked through her curls, forcing her face back. Two seconds later she was being ruthlessly kissed.

She didn't struggle. She couldn't. One of Sophie's arms was all but useless but even if both were uninjured she couldn't fight Reith Kenrick's strength. He held her in a grip of iron and his lips possessed her utterly.

Possessed. . .

That was how she felt. Reith was in control. He could do with her as he willed and there was no way she could stop it. His lips fastened on hers, and his mouth demanded a response with an urgency that was almost a cry from the heart.

What was he doing? Why was he kissing her like this?

The man was kissing her with such ravaging passion that it drew from Sophie a reply she hadn't thought she was capable of feeling. This wasn't the kiss of anger—or of challenge. It was the kiss of a man who was hungering for something he had never had and didn't believe existed. Reith Kenrick might swear he needed no one—but his need was there in his kiss.

It wasn't just a need. It was an overwhelming, insatiable hunger that caught at Sophie's soul.

There was no way she wanted to stop it. To her horror she felt the urgent quiver of response shudder through her body. Reith was right. He just had to touch her and her sensible resolutions were put aside.

Reluctantly but inevitably Sophie's lips parted, answering his need, responding to his urgency. Her soul was caught by him—desperate to appease his hunger in any way she knew how.

Kevin. . .

She had no right to appease this man's hunger when she was firmly affianced. She had no right. . .

The thought flashed through her mind in a jolt of desperate confusion. She jerked back, and, to her bewilderment, she was released.

There was no sound but the jerky, shallow gasps coming from Sophie's lips. Reith was watching her as a hawk might watch a sparrow, only the inner depths of his eyes reflecting a trace of uncertainty behind the cynicism. Sophie was powerless to define her feelings. She stood, hands falling uselessly to her sides, and her wide eyes looked up at Reith in dismay.

'Why. . .why did you do that?' she whispered at last. 'To punish me?'

'What would I punish you for, Sophie Lynton?' Reith asked and to Sophie's amazement Reith's voice was not quite steady. He put a hand out and placed it on her shoulder. 'I'd like to take you to my bed.'

Sophie moistened dry lips. 'I suspect. . .I suspect that your bed would be a pretty lonely place to be—for any woman.'

'You'd like to try?'

'No!'

'How do you know if you won't try?' His eyes were throwing out an enigmatic challenge and Sophie shook her head.

'I guess. . .I guess I'm starting to know you, Reith Kenrick. And I'm starting to think that by your side is a fairly bleak place to be.'

'Why?'

'Because you don't need anyone—except maybe for sexual gratification.'

'And Kevin needs more than that?'

'Yes.' Did he? She wasn't sure.

He must, Sophie thought savagely, twisting the brilliant diamond on her ring finger. He was marrying her, after all, and there were women enough for sex.

Such as the woman laughing behind him on the phone. . .

A wave of doubt and uncertainty—and maybe even pure bleakness—must have crossed her face because the cynicism suddenly faded from Reith's eyes.

'Hey, Sophie,' he said softly. 'I didn't mean to make you unhappy.'

'Well, you have,' Sophie whispered. She took a deep breath, struggling for words. 'Like it or not, Reith Kenrick, you have. Now, if you don't mind, I want to be taken home.'

CHAPTER FIVE

SHE needn't see Reith Kenrick ever again.

Sophie lay in her bed that night and tried desperately to block out the remembrance of Reith's mouth on hers. She failed absolutely.

Kevin was coming. This was Wednesday night. In thirty-six hours she'd have Kevin by her side and Reith Kenrick would fade to a bad memory.

The thought made her twist in her bed with bleak, hopeless longing.

Good grief, Sophie Lynton, you're a twenty-eight-year-old doctor of medicine and you're behaving like some stupid schoolgirl with a crush. Just because you feel sorry for the man. . .

Sorry? Was she sorry for Reith?

It wasn't true. What she felt for Reith Kenrick was empathy—empathy because of her own bleak childhood.

'But I've sorted myself out,' she told the darkness. 'So can Reith Kenrick. He doesn't need me!'

He didn't need anyone.

'Says Reith Kenrick!'

Sophie twisted over and gave her pillow a vicious thump. The man had unsettled her to the point where sleep was impossible. The sooner Kevin arrived and married her out of hand the better.

Only Kevin won't marry me out of hand, she thought sadly. He'll have to fit me into his schedule. . .

Between his women. . .

Stop it, Sophie Lynton. You're being a fool. You have no real reason to think Kevin's unfaithful. If you don't trust him now, what sort of basis is there for a marriage?

67

I do trust him! It was a child's bereft wail and Sophie didn't believe it for a moment.

The telephone's sudden ring resounding shrilly through the dark shook her out of her misery. She buried her face deeper in the pillows while Mrs Sanderson padded down the hall to answer it.

Sophie was still the only guest in the place. Maybe this was more people wanting late accommodation. Being a guest-house proprietor must be almost as bad as being a doctor for late-night calls, Sophie thought ruefully.

It wasn't a guest. A moment later there was a rapid knock on Sophie's door.

'Are you awake, dear?'

'Yes.' Sophie sat up and swore as an alternative reason for the phone call presented itself. Kevin! It had to be Kevin ringing with an excuse as to why he wasn't arriving on Friday.

She flicked on her bedside lamp and glared at her watch. Two a.m. in Australia was late afternoon in Belgium and it wouldn't occur to Kevin to worry about waking Sophie and her landlady. 'I'll bet he hasn't even apologised to Moira,' she muttered savagely as she flung off her bedcover.

'Coming,' she called, but Moira Sanderson was already opening the door.

'Sophie, it's Dr Kenrick,' her landlady faltered, her voice laced with anxiety. 'He needs your help.'

'Help. . .' Sophie stared at Moira for a split-second and then her emergency training slid into place. 'Is he still on the phone?'

'He hung up. Sophie, it's an emergency and he was moving fast. He asked. . .he asked if I could take you over to the Bells' place.'

'The Bells'. . .'

'They live up in the hills behind the town.' Moira Sanderson was talking fast, breathless with urgency. 'Trevor Bell's a single parent and he's odd. He had some sort of breakdown in the city and he brought his little girl to Inyabarra last year. He keeps to himself, but there's talk that he's schizophrenic and the social-welfare people have been concerned about the child. Anyway, I gather their neighbour heard shots a few minutes ago, went over and found the little girl wandering around outside with blood all over her. When Ted, the neighbour, went to the door Trevor Bell shot him in the leg. Now Trevor's barricaded himself in the house and is shooting at anything that moves. Ted's wife called the police and Dr Kenrick. The police are on their way. Dr Kenrick will be there in five minutes but he says by the sound of it he'll need back-up.'

Back-up? Sophie blinked. It sounded as if what Dr Kenrick needed was the army.

'Does he have a nurse to help in emergencies?'

'There's a trained sister who lives in Inyabarra, but she's away visiting her parents in the city.'

'I'll come.' Sophie was already pulling her jeans on.

'You don't need to—'

'You'll never find the place without me,' Moira Sanderson said firmly. 'And Dr Kenrick needs you fast. I can get you there almost as soon as Dr Kenrick arrives—that is, if I don't stop to put on my corset.' She gave the trace of an anxious smile, and Sophie guessed she'd go without more than her corset rather than be left behind. 'I know you're the doctor, dear, but I've lived a good few years in these parts. There's not a lot that can shock me, and I may be able to help.'

By the time they arrived at the Bells' small cottage, there was more than just the wounded neighbour and Reith at the scene. Word had flown round this small community, even at two in the morning. The weather-board cottage was floodlit with lights from the local fire engine. For some reason the fire chief was there in full regalia, standing nervously behind a burly police constable, and a small group of onlookers were clustered around an area where Reith worked.

Moira, splendidly garbed in crimson dressing-gown and curlers—she'd decided that without her corset she might as well stay in what she had on—pushed her way through the lot of them, weaving a path for Sophie.

'Dr Kenrick needs Dr Lynton,' she said loudly. 'Give us room.'

Reith looked up with real relief in his face. He was too preoccupied to so much as glance at the extraordinary Moira. All he saw was Sophie—another pair of trained hands.

'Dr Lynton. . .' It was a momentary acknowledgement of her presence before he turned back to the job. There was no time for pleasantries.

Sophie bent swiftly over the man Reith was working on, her eyes doing a lightning-fast assessment. The ground around them was liberally splattered with blood. Below his thigh, the man's leg was a pulpy mess, and Sophie winced as she realised the extent of the damage.

'A shotgun wound?'

'Mmm.' Reith was packing the wounded flesh hard with wads of dressing, trying desperately to stop the oozing flow of blood. 'I need oxygen, Dr Lynton. In my. . .'

Sophie was already moving, finding Reith's mask and cylinder with ease from the heap of equipment someone had hauled from his car. She adjusted the mask on the man's face, felt his pulse and grimaced. The man was ashen and his pulse was hardly there. He was bleeding to death under their hands.

'Can we shift him head below heart?' She was talking to herself, aware that all of Reith's concentration was in stopping the blood flow. She needed to answer her own question—but how?

She glanced around fast. Someone had produced a pile of thick blankets. Swiftly she folded them into a thick wad, then shoved them beside the injured man from the waist down.

As she worked, she watched Reith, waiting for him to acknowledge what she was doing. Their eyes met for a brief instant, acknowledging their teamwork. Reith was a solid, competent person to work with, Sophie thought fleetingly, remembering some of the bumbling professionals she had worked with in emergencies. There was no need to explain things to Reith. In that brief meeting of their eyes he had acknowledged her efforts and told her he was behind her. 'Now?' she asked.

Reith left his pressure pad for a split-second, moving with Sophie in a swift, professional lift to haul the man's lower body up onto the wedge of blankets. It was not much of a pad, but it was enough to elevate his lower limbs.

Better. Now what blood pressure there was would be aided in getting blood to the brain and hindered in pumping it into the legs—toward the wound and out onto the grass.

'He's lost a massive amount.' Reith was back working on his pressure pad almost before the man was lying on the blankets. 'Can you set up a drip, fast? I'm having trouble staunching the flow.' His eyes signalled to the pile of equipment. 'You'll find everything. . . There's plasma. . .'

Sophie was already moving, searching in Reith's bag for what she needed. The man's pain-dulled eyes followed her.

'Morphine?' she queried. They might as well have been in Casualty, rather than on the leaf-strewn yard of a bush cottage. Their surroundings were blocked out and onlookers ignored. There was only the desperate task at hand. With a wound such as this, the man was lucky to still be alive now. Sophie looked at the extent of the blood around them and grimaced. It gave her a fair idea of the sort of wound under Reith's hands.

'Already administered.' Reith's face was grim and

intent. 'It should take effect in a moment or two.' He touched the man lightly on the hand and then went back to applying pressure. 'You'll feel relief any minute, Ted.'

The man grunted acknowledgement.

'Sophie, there's a child hurt.' Reith's voice was tight with strain and Sophie knew that, although Reith had been forced to give Ted priority treatment, he was still worried about the patient he had left untended. 'As far as I could see on a fast examination, she has a flesh wound, not as serious as this, but she's in shock. Once the drip's set up here I can work on alone while you give her some proper attention. I only gave her a cursory once-over. . .'

Sophie nodded. Reith would have done a rapid triage. . . It was an absolute rule in emergencies that all patients were seen fast before any work was done at all. Triage was the allocation of priorities, and this man's horrendous leg wound would have to be an absolute priority.

Triage wasn't always clear. This time Reith had found his choice obvious, but in an emergency there were often hard decisions to be made. If man and child had both been bleeding to death Reith would have been forced to decide which he was most likely to save, and if both were equally possible then age and all sorts of nebulous factors such as number of dependents came into it.

Dreadful decisions. The sort of decisions Sophie, in a huge London hospital with back-up teams and other hospitals minutes away, never had to face. But a lone doctor like Reith. . . It was an awesome responsibility.

'How old's the child?' Sophie asked.

'Four.' Reith was still desperately fighting the blood flow. 'I need more wadding, Dr Lynton. Hell, there's not nearly enough here.' There was the edge of desperation in his voice, as if he was losing the fight. Sophie badly wanted to help him, but she had to get the drip running first. It was her job to replace the plasma. Priorities. . .

She inserted the intravenous needle for the drip quickly, thanking her stars for the man's lean, work-worn hands with veins that etched themselves like lines on a contour map. Moments later the plasma bottle and tubing were attached.

'Plasma's going through now,' Sophie told Reith as she taped the drip onto the back of the man's hand and watched the thick fluid start dripping into the vein. Usually in this situation they had to use saline, but Reith had come prepared. Plasma until they could cross match his blood.

Plasma wasn't usually found in doctors' surgeries but then Reith Kenrick's surgery was no ordinary clinic. Reith Kenrick was no ordinary doctor. . .

Now she could concentrate on Reith's needs. Wadding. . . She looked around the group of open-mouthed neighbours. If they had to have spectators then the spectators might as well make themselves useful.

'I want shirts,' she said. Behind her, the crimson Moira was doing her best to comfort a sobbing woman in the crowd. Moira looked up and her eyes questioned Sophie. 'Moira, can you organise any man wearing a soft shirt or singlet—or woman wearing cotton or cotton-mix lingerie? I want them now!'

'Sure—'

A shotgun blast from the house made them all jump. The onlookers moved nervously back, and Moira moved among them, bullying the shirts from their backs. Then, with a defiant glance across to the house—as if to say, Shoot me if you dare—she stalked across and handed them to Sophie.

'Is there a problem with the woman?' Sophie asked. The woman Moira had been attending was now threatening hysterics.

'If I had a bucket of water handy I'd toss it over

her,' Moira said darkly. 'Elvira Pilkington lives four doors down and is only here to get maximum drama. If nothing happens she'll invent the drama herself. What else needs doing, Sophie?'

'Could you find out where the wounded child is?'

Moira nodded, the amazing crimson dressing-gown moving off with purpose. The curlers bobbed all the way out of floodlight range.

'Did I ask if we're out of range of the gun?' Sophie asked Reith as she ripped the shirts into manageable sections. Tomorrow she'd have to account for these, she knew. From Casualty experience, Sophie knew to destroy people's possessions, no matter how grave the emergency, always led to trouble. Tomorrow she or Reith would have to face at least one person claiming that she'd torn his most expensive shirt and was she going to pay for it or did she prefer to listen to a lawyer? Reith gave a strained smile.

'Yeah. The good thing about shotguns is they haven't the range of rifles, and Ted here says Trevor's only got a shotgun.'

Ted. . . Their patient. . .

Ted was trying to talk now, fighting off the oxygen mask. Sophie lifted it slightly and bent to listen.

'He's a mad bastard,' the injured neighbour whispered through gritted teeth. 'Threatened to shoot me a few weeks ago because one of his chooks wandered over to my place. I took the thing back and the crazy coot threatened to shoot me if I came near the place again. And tonight I took his daughter back. . .'

His words trailed off to a pain-filled gasp and Sophie felt his pulse. What she felt reassured her. It was still faint but steadying. If only Reith could stop the blood flow. . .

'Got it,' Reith said harshly. He looked up to Sophie. She was adjusting the drip rate to maximum. 'Blood flow's stopped. I need some tape to hold all this in position.'

Reith needed a theatre nurse in this improvised theatre. Sophie finished what she was doing, fished in his bag for tape, cut lengths and handed them across.

'Is there any medical help within reach?' she asked as he taped. She didn't want to ask what was really in her mind while Ted was still conscious and listening, but with a wound like this the blood circulation to the leg would be cut. Ted would need vascular surgery and grafting within hours if he wasn't to lose the leg. 'An ambulance?'

'I've got the fire chief to radio Melbourne for the air ambulance,' Reith said grimly. 'They're locating the nearest one now. At most they'll take an hour to get here and an hour back to Melbourne—providing we don't have to wait for more patients.'

Sophie nodded. She stood, casting a nervous glance across at the cottage. There were no lights—nothing. Only someone standing behind closed curtains with a loaded shotgun. . .

Would it be better just to leave him alone with his shotgun—get all of these people out of here and wait for sanity to return?

It was a decision for the police, and one Sophie didn't envy them. On the one hand, patience could mean less bloodshed. On the other—if they left him be and he stormed out into neighbours' homes. . .

That was the police constable's job. The policeman was behind his car, closest of all of them to the house, and as Sophie glanced across she saw him raise a megaphone. How to talk to a madman. . .

'I'll check the child.' She looked down at Reith's long fingers carefully adjusting the tape. Reith couldn't leave yet. With a wound like this and a drip in place at least one of them had to stay in attendance—at least until they were sure the bleeding had stopped for good.

'I wish you would. . .'

Moira had found the child. As Sophie stood, uncertain of where to go, the brilliant dressing-gown and curlers bobbed out from the trees and signalled Sophie.

'Mandy's over here, Sophie. Mrs Vickers—Ted's wife—has her next door, out of sight of the cottage.'

An excellent idea. Sophie blinked at the coolness of Mrs Vickers—to leave her injured husband in Reith's care and think calmly enough to remove the child from view.

It was important. If the man doing the shooting was the child's father and he emerged from the cottage shooting. . . Well, it certainly wasn't the place for his four-year-old daughter.

Sophie slipped through the undergrowth at the bottom of the cottage garden, following the redoubtable Moira. It was a clear moonlit night, which was lucky, as Sophie didn't have a torch. As it was, she stumbled through the overgrown garden.

Not Moira, though. The corsetless Moira was in her element. She reached the fence between the two houses, hitched up her dressing-gown, hoisted her legs over and stood and waited for Sophie.

'Do you want a hand?' she asked Sophie kindly and Sophie shook her head.

'I can manage,' she said faintly. It was a three-foot fence and Moira had scaled it with the agility of a ten-year-old.

The child Sophie was looking for was on the neighbours' veranda, cradled in the arms of a gaunt woman in her late thirties. Both woman and child were in nightclothes, and there was blood over both nightgowns.

'Sophie, this is Mary Vickers, Ted's wife,' Moira said briefly as she and Sophie walked up the front steps to the lighted front veranda. Sophie nodded in greeting. The woman's face was set hard, in an expressionless glaze of fear. She was hugging the child to her as if desperate for contact. 'And Mandy.'

Triage. . . Sophie glanced at the bloom of blood on

the child's shoulder. The nightgown had been torn away to reveal a flesh wound, bleeding sluggishly but almost stopped. By the look of it, the shotgun pellets had merely grazed the flesh. Mary Vickers, though. . . She looked as though she would topple over at any moment.

Sophie touched the woman's face gently with her fingers and knelt until she was looking straight into the woman's agony-filled eyes.

'Are you hurt?' she asked gently. 'Is any of this blood yours?'

'It's Ted's.' Mary Vickers' voice was a harsh, agonised whisper. 'I held him until. . .until Dr Kenrick arrived.'

So it was only fear. . .

'Mary, Ted's going to be OK,' Sophie said firmly. 'Dr Kenrick's stopped the bleeding, and is dressing Ted's leg now. We've called the air ambulance from Melbourne because the shotgun pellets have damaged the artery—he'll have to have an operation tonight to repair it—but Ted's pulse is steady, we've set up a drip to replace the blood he's lost and he definitely will live.'

Ted might end up losing his leg, but this wasn't the time to say that.

Mary Vickers stared at Sophie for a long, long moment. The terror-filled glaze slowly died from her eyes and they focused.

'R-really?'

'I promise.'

The woman burst into tears.

There hadn't been a sound from Mandy. Now Sophie lifted the child away from the weeping woman, leaving the way for Moira to enfold Mary in all-enveloping crimson comfort. The child came unresisting into Sophie's arms, too shocked to resist.

Sophie swiftly checked her and then nodded to Moira. 'I can manage here, Moira.' She'd have to

check the wound and make sure there was nothing else
wrong, but she could do that by herself. 'Would you
take Mary back to her husband?' Mary Vickers needed
to see her husband recovering his colour almost as
much as Ted Vickers would need Mary, Sophie
thought.

Mary Vickers dragged herself to her feet. 'I'd. . .
I'd like that. I wanted to stay. . .but when Dr Kenrick
arrived and took over looking after Ted I knew I had
to take Mandy away. . .I was so frightened someone
else would get shot and the little one was there. . .
She's just a baby. . .'

And no one else would help. Sophie bit her lip.
There were two types of people in an emergency—
those who did what had to be done, like Moira and
Mary Vickers, and those who came to gape and
wonder. Take photographs while people died around
them. . .

Sophie gathered the limp child to her. 'Can I take
her inside, Mary?'

'Sure—'

Mary's word was cut off short. There was a shout
of horror from the next-door garden, lights blazed out,
a blast of gunshot, then a short, staccato command
boomed through the megaphone.

'Don't be a bloody fool. Stop, man—'

Then suddenly Reith's voice, as though the megaphone had been wrenched from the policeman.

Instead of urgency, Reith's voice held calm—as
though there was all the time in the world.

'Trevor, we're not here to harm you. No one's going
to hurt you. The only reason we're here is that you've
got a gun and everyone's nervous, but we're here to
help you. You know me, Trev. I'm the local doctor.
I'm not a policeman. There's no need to shoot.

'Mandy's out here, Trevor. Your little girl. She's
hurt but she's OK. She needs you, Trevor. She's asking
for you. Trevor, put down the gun and come—'

The words were cut off by a savage, explosive blast of gunfire.

Then silence.

Reith. . .

Mary Vickers was the first to break the horrified silence on the veranda. 'Oh, God. . . Ted. . .' The woman gave a sob of despair and took off in a desperate run through the darkened garden.

Moira looked wildly around at Sophie. One curler had come askew and was dangling crazily over her eyes, and as she shoved it back another fell down to roll uselessly away down the veranda steps.

'Will I look after Mandy?' Moira whispered in breathless horror.

The little girl had gone rigid in Sophie's clasp. Sophie felt for her pulse. Shock had taken its toll. She hadn't examined her. She didn't know for sure there was no other wound. She couldn't leave her. . .

'Go with Mary, Moira,' Sophie said harshly. 'And come back fast.'

'But if he's shot Doc Kenrick. . . It sounded like—'

'Then yell for dear life and I'll come. Go!'

Reith Kenrick had been behind the megaphone when Trevor had shot. Maybe he was still out of range, but it sounded as if the man had emerged, gun blazing. The obvious target for a shooter was the man behind the megaphone. Reith. . .

Sophie's heart lurched in sickening dread and the child moved convulsively in her arms, sensing her panic.

Mandy. . . Concentrate on Mandy. . .

'Hush,' she told the little girl in her arms, and it was the hardest thing she had ever done, to keep her voice even and free of horror. 'There's nothing wrong. I think your daddy's shooting things with a gun. He shot you by mistake, but I guess he's out shooting rabbits or something else now.' How to say that and make it sound completely normal? Somehow she did.

'Now, Mandy, let's get you inside and warm, and find
something to put on your sore arm.'

Reith. . .

Your priority is this little one, Sophie Lynton, she
told herself harshly. Until they come back and tell you
otherwise, your priority is Mandy.

CHAPTER SIX

BAD news travels fast. Sophie told herself that over and over in the endless minutes as she carried the child inside and carefully examined and soothed her. There was no more sound of gunshots.

Surely the silence was a good sign? If there was bad news, surely Moira or someone else would burst through the trees and tell her she was needed?

Or they're all dead. . .

Crazy thought. Concentrate on Mandy. No news is good news. . .

The arm was the only wound on the child except for one dark bruise on her back. The bruise was recent—inflicted in the last twenty-four hours. Mandy didn't speak—just lay, limp again and lifeless, her tiny eyes reflecting the night's horror.

Sophie found milk in the kitchen. Leaving Mandy huddled in blankets by the stove, her huge eyes watching her as she worked, Sophie carefully warmed it and then found chocolate to sweeten it. It was simple work, but getting fluids into Mandy would alleviate the shock, and administering them to a frightened child via mouth was more comforting, and infinitely preferable if she could manage it, than the strangeness of a drip. There had been little blood loss. It was only fear that was causing the shock.

It was comforting to make the hot chocolate too, normal action blotting out in part fear of what lay outside. Domesticity as a shield to horror. If they needed her they'd be back by now, Sophie thought. If they weren't all dead.

No news is good news. . .

Sophie knelt by Mandy and held the mug to her

81

lips. To her surprise, the child reached out and grasped it, gulping it down with a thirst that made Sophie's eyes widen.

'M. . .more,' the child whispered and held out the empty mug.

'Are you hungry, little one?' Sophie asked, filling the pan with more milk.

'Daddy wouldn't let me have tea. Or lunch. He hit me and made me cry. Daddy. . .' Her voice faded again, fear taking over.

'Mandy, it sounds like your daddy is ill,' Sophie said gently. 'Sometimes, when people are ill, they do things that they don't want to do. If your daddy's head was hurting, maybe he wouldn't even know he was hurting you.'

'My daddy has to take pills,' Mandy said seriously. 'Every day.'

'Has he been taking his pills lately?'

The child's fearful eyes focused on Sophie. 'I don't. . .I don't think so.'

'Then I think that's what's wrong,' Sophie told her. 'I'm a doctor, Sophie, and I think what's wrong with your dad is a sickness, just like a horrid, sniffly cold. When your Daddy's not taking his pills then his head doesn't work properly. I think when he hit you and shot at you—maybe he really did think you were a rabbit and not his beloved little Mandy.'

'I think so too,' Mandy whispered in a tiny voice. 'He wouldn't shoot me.'

'Of course he wouldn't.'

Two more huge mugs of chocolate and the edge of fear faded from the child's eyes. The warmth from the stove and blankets was creeping through her body. Her eyelids drooped over the horror. She jerked herself into wakefulness once, twice, and then it was too much.

She slept.

When she was sure Mandy's sleep was deep and not

likely to end, Sophie finally let herself walk out onto the veranda. The place was as quiet as death. Nothing moved.

Maybe he'd shot everyone, she thought. Maybe even now he was down there in the undergrowth. . .

Nightmare scenario. Impossible. There hadn't been enough gunshots. There had been no gunshots since Mary and Moira had left.

So why didn't someone come?

The urge to leave the sleeping child was almost overwhelming but Sophie refused to give in to it. If Mandy's father had shot her and Mandy's father was indeed out there. . .

There was no sound. The wind had come up and was blowing enough to disguise the sound of cars and normal voices in next door's garden. Someone must come soon and tell her what was going on. She was going mad.

Then, above her head, she heard the distant noise of a helicopter, growing louder. Once again floodlights flashed out from next door, this time aimed into the sky and then down, as if to show a clearing. Sophie took a sobbing breath of thankfulness. At least someone else was alive in the nightmare.

It was a massive helicopter, sent by the army, by the look of the painted insignia showing in the floodlight. Reith has the army he needs, Sophie told herself firmly and crossed everything she possessed in the hope that he was able to appreciate it.

Still no one came. The helicopter hovered, obviously waiting for the locals to light flares and signal a safe place to land. It finally descended on the other side of the neighbouring house.

There was silence again for five minutes. Five minutes stretched to ten, and Sophie's nerves were stretched to breaking. Then, with a reverberating clamour, the machine roared into life and rose high into the night sky. It moved fast, disappearing into the distance until its light was just another star in the night sky.

And still Sophie stood, staring out into the mind-numbing darkness. She was going mad. . . Casualty in London was never like this. How much longer could she hold her breath?

And finally he came, not Mary or Moira, but Reith himself, striding swiftly up through the garden as though it weren't night and the garden weren't over-grown. For a moment Sophie wasn't sure—but her eyes had adjusted to the darkness and as he appeared in the moonlight she'd have known his lean, athletic figure anywhere.

Sophie gave a sob of pure relief and then her hands gripped the balustrade of the steps hard. Her knees were water. Reith was alive, and for some crazy, crazy reason that was all that mattered. Reith. . .

Reith stopped at the base of the steps. He stood, looking up at her, and in his eyes she saw the same horror she had seen in Mary's, and Mandy's—and maybe it was even reflected in her own eyes. Sophie clutched the balustrade for all she was worth and made herself speak

'What. . .what's happened?'

'He's dead.' Reith's voice was flat and emotionless—the voice of a surgeon who had just lost a patient after long hours of heartbreaking surgery, or a doctor who had just lost a child after months of cancer. The voice of a doctor who cared so much that it was eating into his soul.

'He. . .he killed himself?'

'No.' Reith shook his head, indescribably weary. 'He came out shooting, walking straight for us, shooting all the time. The police constable killed him. He had no choice.'

His words were flat, emotionless fact. Only the horror in his eyes gave him away.

Silence. The horror grew and grew, and Reith's face stayed rigid with self-control.

And suddenly Sophie could bear it no longer. She walked slowly down the steps, twisted her hands around his neck and pulled Reith Kenrick's head down to her breast.

For one long minute Reith stayed rigid, the self-control fighting, fighting for supremacy. Then she felt his rigid body give a long, long shudder of release, and Reith pulled her into him as though he were a man drowning.

It must have been ten long minutes before they surfaced. They stayed together for what seemed eternity. Neither wished to break the moment. Closeness was all that mattered.

Reith was safe. He was alive and Sophie knew she hadn't realised how much she cared until that moment. Until now. Until he was less than a heartbeat away and his heart was beating in tandem with hers with a strength that made her own heart dissolve in gratitude and. . .

And love. Love. . .

What was she thinking? How could she love a man she had known for less than a week?

She could hardly form the thought. There was only the moment. There was only now—and the wonder of the warmth flooding through her body.

There was wonder in the way he was holding her. There was wonder in the feeling surging around her heart. It was a feeling she had never known before— a feeling she hadn't known existed.

It was a feeling that she had found her home. . . her heart. . .that this heart beating so strongly against hers was part and parcel of hers—that to separate his heart from hers would require something sharper than a scalpel.

'Sophie. . .' Reith's lips were in her hair, and his hands held her close, seeking comfort from the horror.

There was nothing more than that need in his hold, Sophie told herself harshly. Nothing more.

Finally, unwillingly, Reith drew away, holding Sophie at arm's length and looking down into her face with concern.

'I dragged you into a nightmare.'

'The nightmare was yours,' she said gently. 'I wish. . . I wish I could have done more. If you knew how helpless I felt—being here. . .'

'You helped save Ted's life. It was touch and go when you came. If I hadn't had your help. . .'

His voice dragged to an exhausted halt. Reith put a hand to his face as though wiping away thoughts that were too dreadful to face. Sophie had to physically hold herself back from reaching out to hold him once again. His need was almost a tangible thing, and her need matched his.

'Mandy,' he said at last. 'What's the damage?'

'She's asleep,' Sophie said gently. 'The pellets just grazed her shoulder and there's no other significant injury. She's been lucky.'

Reith shook his head. 'She's been abysmally unlucky. To lose her dad. . .' Once more that hand moved to his face in a gesture of exhaustion. 'I should have stepped in earlier.'

'You knew there was trouble?'

'Trevor's been under psychiatric care for years but refuses to take medication. His wife walked out when Mandy was a baby—who could blame her? But I do blame her for not taking Mandy. There was an incident in the city that made Social Welfare move in and threaten to take Mandy into foster care, and when things settled down Trevor moved here. The authorities contacted me and asked me to keep an eye on things. I tried. . . God knows, I tried. He seemed stable—only just but not unbalanced enough to justify removing Mandy. And he certainly loved her. . .'

His face closed in pain and Sophie nodded in slow

comprehension. Every doctor's nightmare—deciding when to suggest the risk was great enough to remove a child from a parent.

'I didn't think he'd hurt Mandy,' Reith said. 'He had a shock when they threatened to take Mandy away in the city and I'm sure he hasn't touched her. Heaven knows, I've watched the child, dropping in on the slightest pretext.'

'There's bruising on her back,' Sophie told him. 'Only the one bruise, though.'

'I wonder whether that was what finally drove him over the edge,' Reith said flatly. 'If he struck Mandy then he would have horrified himself. He was terrified of Social Welfare. He wasn't going to let them have Mandy—no matter what—and if they knew he'd struck Mandy. . . Well, maybe his mad brain thought she might as well be dead.'

'Poor little mite.' Sophie was watching Reith's face, seeing the pain for other people's agony etched deep. It was a lie that this man wasn't involved with people. She sighed, aware suddenly of an almost overwhelming weariness. 'What happens now?'

'We lock up here and take Mandy home.'

'Home?' Sophie flashed Reith a startled look. There was no going home for Mandy.

'To your home,' Reith said. 'Or, rather, the guest house.' He shrugged. 'I forgot—you won't know what's happened, how we've tied the ends up for the night. It seems the army reserve is running field exercises thirty miles from here. When all hell broke loose the police sent for back-up. They sent their field ambulance—the helicopter. It's taken Ted and his wife off to Melbourne. The police are still busy in the cottage, but I've certified Trevor dead and my job's over. Now. . .now I've talked Moira into having Mandy for a while—not that it took much persuasion.'

'Wouldn't Mandy be best being sent to Melbourne? Are there any relations?'

'None, as far as I know. Social Welfare have been trying to contact her mother for years with no success.' Reith sighed and ran his hand through his hair. 'But I've an idea about her long-term care.' He shrugged. 'It may come to nothing but if she's shuttled off to foster care in Melbourne then she's lost another chance.'

'You do care about her, don't you?'

'She's a nice little kid. If they can't find her mother, and I don't see how they can succeed now, then she's faced with not being able to be adopted. Even at four she looked after her dad when he was moody and irrational. She deserves parents.' He shook his head. 'Let's lock up here and get her back to Moira's. She's gone ahead to have a bed ready—took a few of Mandy's toys and things.'

Who thought of that? Sophie thought, startled, and knew instinctively that it was this man. Reith Kenrick was starting to have depths she hadn't known. Depths she hadn't known in any man. . .

Moira was waiting for them on the guest-house veranda, still resplendent in crimson. Her curlers, Sophie was pleased to see, had been taken out. With the bouncing they'd received tonight Sophie had thought they'd be so twisted they'd have to be cut out.

'Bring her upstairs,' Moira told Reith as he lifted the sleeping little girl from the car. She cast a quick, concerned glance at Sophie. 'I've put her next to you, Sophie. There's an adjoining room.' She blinked. 'I'd put her in with me but I sleep like the dead—if she wakes I mightn't hear.'

'That's fine by me,' Sophie told her. 'I'll wake if she does.'

'Well, I'm not charging you for tonight's accommodation,' Moira said roundly. 'Not if you're acting nursemaid.'

'I don't mind,' Sophie told her, following Reith into the house. She shrugged and a small smile washed across her face. 'Dr Kenrick told me my bill for his services would be large. It seems he wasn't exaggerating.'

To her surprise Reith turned and flashed her a smile. The smile lit his face, glinting deep within his eyes, and the smile made Sophie gasp. It was a caress in itself. It took away some of the horror of the past few hours and lit her within.

Reith Kenrick. . . Something inside Sophie was growing with the speed of a bushfire. Something she didn't have any control over.

It frightened the life out of her.

She looked away from him but Reith must have seen the flickering look of fear. He slowed his steps, waiting for her to come up to him.

'What's wrong, Sophie?'

'N-nothng,' she whispered. 'It's just. . .it's just been a long day.'

'You've had longer days than this in Casualty. Unless the English medical system treats its juniors kinder than the Australian one does.'

'I know,' Sophie agreed. 'I'm just out of practice.'

It wasn't true. She could stay up all night and still operate near to capacity the next day—it was something most doctors learned to do very early in their careers.

What she couldn't do was cope with the emotional rollercoaster she was on now. It was something she had never had to deal with, and wasn't sure she wanted to know how.

They tucked Sophie into bed, opened the door to Sophie's room and then Moira tiptoed off to her own bed.

'I don't know about you two young things,' she told them, 'but I'm exhausted. I don't know how I'll sleep after the. . .after the goings-on tonight, but I'll sure give it a try.'

Sophie and Reith stood looking after her. The traces

of a smile were still playing around Reith's mouth.

'Redoubtable lady,' he said softly and Sophie smiled in agreement.

It was crazily intimate to stand in this darkened bed-room with Reith beside her. There was a bedlight in the corner playing a soft glow over the sleeping child, but that was all.

'She is that.' She looked down at the sleeping Mandy. 'Reith, if you're thinking Moira can look after Mandy long-term—'

'I'm not,' he told her, seeing the doubt on her face. 'Moira Sanderson is some lady, but taking on a four-year-old at sixty is no mean task. It's Ted and Mary Vickers I'm thinking of.'

The Vickerses. . . Sophie thought back to the hag-gard lady she had seen that night and her wounded husband, and a small crease played around her eyes. 'Do you have any reason for suggesting them?'

'I have about ten.'

'But you're keeping them to yourself.'

Reith grinned. 'I guess I'm not used to sharing my professional thoughts with a colleague.' He shrugged. 'A novelty.' He touched her face with his finger and could hardly have known the effect his touch had on her. It was all Sophie could do to conceal the tremor that ran from head to toe.

'So. . .so tell me.'

'Simple, really,' he said. 'Mary and Ted have been trying to have children for years. They're stable, happy, not very well off—but that's no bar to being great parents—and they love kids. They've both loved having Mandy living next door. Sadly, Mary's infertile. They're not suitable for IV techniques, and they've been categorised as too old to adopt. I don't know what the waiting list for adoption's like in your country but here it's impossible.'

'And you think they'll want Mandy.'

'Lots of adoptive parents would want Mandy,' Reith

said. 'She's a great little kid, maybe scarred by what happened tonight but young enough to heal with love. Ted and Mary, though—well, Mandy's been in and out of Mary's kitchen since they moved here. The number of times Mary's been in my clinic worrying about what was happening to Mandy. . . One of the reasons I let Mandy stay with her father was that I knew Mary was next door keeping an eye on things.'

'And you think they might want her long-term?'

'The problem won't be Mary and Ted, but Social Welfare,' Reith said. 'Ted and Mary aren't blood relatives, and there's no reason for them to get favourable treatment—unless I can prove fast that there's a strong emotional bond already. If Ted's surgery goes well Mary will be back here in a couple of days. They run a small farmlet and there are animals to look after. By the time I contact Social Welfare about Mandy, I want Mandy to be ensconced in Mary's kitchen, in an environment where she already feels secure and loved and where her dad's going to be talked about with love and sympathy. I don't think we could do any better than that for Mandy, do you?'

'N—no,' Sophie said wonderingly and looked up at Reith in amazement. 'Did you think all that up before the helicopter took Ted and Mary away? Before you made a decision not to send Mandy?'

'Pretty much.' Reith smiled. 'Even when she was scared out of her wits about Ted, Mary had the time to be anxious about Mandy's fate. I was going to suggest Mandy go in the helicopter too and then realised that Social Welfare would have to collect her as soon as she arrived in Melbourne, and things sort of fell into place.'

'You're quite some doctor, Reith Kenrick,' Sophie said softly. 'You know that?'

'Mutual-admiration society,' Reith told her, his hands reaching out to take hers in the night. 'Thank you for helping tonight, Sophie. It made a difference.'

A difference? To what? To the outcome for Ted Vickers? Or to Sophie's future?

The night was warm around them. The horrors of the night faded to nothing. Beside them Mandy slept on, losing in slumber the emptiness waiting for her in the morning.

Not complete emptiness, Sophie thought. Because of this man. This man who cared. . .

Her heart twisted inside her. She reached up and touched Reith lightly on the lips with hers.

'I think you're wonderful,' she whispered. She couldn't help herself. The words came from within of their own accord and Sophie could no more prevent them than fly.

There was a long, long silence. The world, it seemed, held its breath and Sophie's was held with it. She so wanted a response from this man, and finally she achieved it. With a sigh that was almost a groan he pulled her into his arms and kissed her as she wanted, as she ached to be kissed.

The sweetness was indescribable. There was passion behind the kiss, but it was first and foremost a kiss of affirmation—affirmation of a bond that was growing stronger by the moment. Could he feel it? Sophie wondered. Did Reith Kenrick's heart reach out to touch hers as hers melted toward him?

She put her arms around him, feeling the muscles of his broad back through the thick cotton of his shirt and revelling in the feel. She smelt the masculine smell of him and gloried in it. She wanted him so much. She wanted him closer to her than she had ever wanted a man in her life before. . .

'Sophie. . .' He broke off to breathe her name and then deepened his kiss. Like hers, his hands were exploring the contours of her back, running down over her slim hips, holding her hard against him. His lips devoured her and she sank closer, closer. . .

His fingers came around to unfasten the buttons of

her blouse, lifting to cup the swelling mounds of her breasts. She'd dressed in a rush and hadn't bothered with the confines of a bra, and his fingers revelled in the freedom of her breasts, fingering each nipple in turn until she gasped with pure pleasure. Her body writhed against him, declaring its need with a sureness that she couldn't regret.

What was she? Some sort of wanton hussy, making love to this man with a passion that matched his? She didn't care. She couldn't. All she knew was that she wanted this man as she had never wanted anything in her life before and she was fighting with everything she possessed.

He pushed her away then, holding her at arm's length and looking down at her with the twisted, enigmatic smile that made Sophie melt inside. She tried to return the smile, but her look was all love—heaven knew if she was smiling as well. Her eyes were two flames of dark desire that matched his own.

'Can I take you to bed, my Sophie?' he murmured, his fingers coming up to brush lightly through her curls. 'Will you let me love you?'

Love. . . Was that what he was offering?

'I'm starting to think. . .' Sophie's voice was the thread of a whisper, hoarse with desire. 'I'm starting to think, Reith Kenrick, that I want you as much as you seem to want me.'

The smile twisted further. 'Regardless of the absent Kevin?'

Kevin. . .

Sophie licked suddenly dry lips, a wave of doubt sweeping over her at the lightness of his asking. What was Reith saying? That she was being unfaithful but he didn't mind? That he would love her tonight and then hand her back to Kevin on Friday as used property?

'I guess. . .I guess. . .' she whispered through lips

that would hardly move. 'I guess I have to let Kevin know I've made a mistake.'

There was a long, long silence. The twisted smile slowly disappeared and Reith's eyes became expressionless.

'Sophie, I'm not offering you marriage,' he said slowly. 'I want, badly, to make love to you, but I'm offering you no long-term commitment. Not now. Not ever. I don't want you breaking off an engagement because of me.'

'Then what are you suggesting?' A wave of cold washed through Sophie so thoroughly that she felt herself tremble. 'That I make love to you and then go off and marry Kevin, regardless?'

'What you do long-term is no concern of mine.'

There had never been crueller words. A vice was closing on Sophie's heart.

'You. . .you think I'd do that?' she whispered. 'Make love to you and then marry Kevin as though nothing had changed?'

'Nothing has changed, Sophie. Just because we want each other now—it means nothing. Tomorrow there'll be nothing.'

'Is that what you believe?'

'It's the truth.'

Sophie closed her eyes. She took a step back, trying to move away—and feeling the pain of the scalpel. This man was so scarred by his past. . . She could never reach him. How on earth had she thought she could ever try?

'I think you'd better leave,' she whispered and the words were a physical agony.

'Because I won't promise marriage?'

Sophie shook her head. 'I don't want marriage, Reith Kenrick. Believe it or not, I want you. And if you think that tomorrow there'll be nothing then. . . then you're right. In the morning. . .in the morning I'd have known I'd done the wrong thing. So. . .so

I'm engaged to another man, Reith Kenrick; you've reminded me of that just in time. So will you please leave? Now.'

'You mean that?'

'Yes.'

He nodded. 'Maybe it's best at that,' he said simply, and only his eyes showed regret. He shook his head, as though ridding himself of a feeling he didn't understand. 'God knows, Sophie, I don't want to hurt you.'

'Just go.'

CHAPTER SEVEN

IT WAS a dreadful night. Somewhere toward dawn Sophie drifted into troubled slumber but woke feeling as if she'd had no sleep at all.

Through the open door Sophie could see Mandy stirring. She rose swiftly, gathering Mandy close and taking her back to her big bed as confusion and doubt flooded into the little face. The child looked up with eyes troubled by what seemed a bad dream.

'I want my daddy,' she said in a trembling voice. 'Or my Margy and Ted. . .'

It took time to settle the child, to talk through what had happened in the night, to achieve a measure of calm and finally to bring a tremulous smile to those pale cheeks. By the time she succeeded, Sophie was starting to think Reith was right: Mary and Ted Vickers were obviously more than neighbours to this child.

'May it work,' she whispered to herself as she nestled down in bed with the child curled in the crook of her arm. 'May Ted and Mary want her. May her future be secure. . .'

And what of Sophie's future? Her plans with Kevin were in turmoil and as far as she knew Kevin was on the plane right now, winging his way to Australia to marry his devoted bride.

'But I'm not Kevin's bride,' she whispered to herself, another image flitting through her mind—the painting in Reith's living-room-cum-studio. . . Bush bride. . . That was what she wanted to be.

I could do better than Reith's mother, she told herself. If only. . .

If only Reith would give her the chance. If only

Reith would let down the barriers and expose himself to love.

What chance was there? One in a billion, she told herself bleakly, and then looked up as a beaming Moira came into the room bearing a loaded breakfast tray.

'So you're awake, you pair of sleepyheads. It's about time—another hour and I'd have brought you lunch.'

To her delight, Sophie heard Mandy give a soft chuckle. The resilience of children never ceased to amaze, she thought.

They sat up in bed, Moira ensconced in the armchair beside them, to demolish fried eggs and bacon, toast lavishly spread with bluegum honey, fresh squeezed orange juice, hot chocolate and brewed coffee.

'You two match,' Moira announced to the pair of them, looking at Sophie's and Mandy's bare bandaged arms.

'We've been in the wars,' Sophie agreed.

'What happened to you?' Mandy asked shyly.

'I tried to lift a koala.'

Mandy shook her head in disgust, her opinion of this pretty lady doctor obviously taking a dive. 'You dingaling!'

They all laughed, and Sophie gave her a hard hug. The child would be OK.

It was confirmed a moment later.

'Mary Vickers has been on the phone,' Moira told them.

'My Mary?' Mandy looked up with interest.

'Your Mary,' Moira agreed. 'She rang to say Ted was operated on last night and the surgeons are confident they've saved his leg. She rang, though, because she was worried about you, Miss Mandy. She said she thinks it's best for you to stay here with me until she gets back to Inyabarra, and then she'll take you home. That's fine with me if it's OK with you.'

'That's OK.' Mandy swung her small toes out of bed. 'I'm going to get dressed now, Mrs Sanderson.

Then can I go and talk to your cat?'

Moira chuckled ruefully as the child walked out of the door. 'She knows this place—but heaven, Sophie, I thought she'd be a lot more upset than this.'

'She's not really facing it yet,' Sophie told her. 'She asked once whether her father was dead but was hardly interested in my reply. Small children are good at facing only what they're strong enough to cope with. It'll be up to Mary and Ted to gradually teach her to live with what's happened.' Sophie frowned. 'Not that the next few days—week, really—won't be hard. She won't be able to block everything out, and I'd guess there'll be a few dreadful times before she comes to terms with it. If she's uncertain or lonely or insecure. . .'

'I'll have her stick by me,' Moira promised. 'Only. . .' Her face clouded. 'I'll worry about her in the night after you leave.'

'What if I stay until Mary returns?' Sophie suggested.

'Won't your Kevin have something to say about that?'

Kevin. . .

Kevin was becoming not her security but an obstacle in her life. Was Kevin on the plane even as they spoke? What on earth was Sophie to do about Kevin?

'We agreed to stay here a week together,' Sophie said doubtfully. 'Just because Kevin's late doesn't mean we should change that, so we'll stay a week from the time he arrives.'

Only she didn't want him to arrive. She wanted Reith. . .

'So what will we do with our Mandy today?' she thought out loud, pushing both men firmly out of her head.

'I'm preserving apricots and she can help.'

It sounded good to Sophie. A way to occupy the mind—to keep it from Reith. 'Sure.'

The telephone interrupted them. Moira departed to answer it.

'For you,' she called, and then destroyed Sophie's calm by calling out, 'It's Dr Kenrick.'

It was hard for Sophie to keep her voice calm as she picked up the telephone and greeted the man on the other end. Reith Kenrick, on the other hand, was having no such trouble. He sounded as if there was nothing between them at all. Tomorrow there would be nothing. Not ever. Cool, calm and professional.

'Is Mandy OK?' he asked.

'She's fine. Mary Vickers rang from Melbourne. . .'

'She rang me too. Sophie, I phoned to remind you about lunch.'

'Lunch?' A flare of absurd hope flickered in Sophie's heart, only to die with Reith's next words.

'With Mrs Lee. Remember, she invited you for lunch? I think it's important you still go.'

'You're going to get maximum use out of me while I'm here,' Sophie snapped, anger flaring. That he could kiss her as he had and then calmly talk as if there was nothing between them. . .'What a waste that I won't go to bed with you as well.'

Sophie bit her tongue on the words. What a dreadful thing to say. What a dreadful thing to think!

'I'll ring her and tell her you're not coming, shall I?' Reith demanded and his voice was cold as he ignored what she had just said. Emotional outbursts, it seemed, were not Reith Kenrick's forte.

'I'll go.' She could match him for coldness. 'I said I would.'

'If you feel under an obligation there's no need—'

'It's got nothing to do with your need, Reith Kenrick,' Sophie snapped. 'I accepted an invitation from Margaret Lee and I intend to keep it. Who knows, if she'd got it in for you I might just find myself wholeheartedly agreeing with her sentiments?'

That was stupid. Sophie replaced the receiver with

trembling fingers. The man was properly under her skin, forcing her to behave in a way she abhorred. Somehow she had to fight for some of Reith's detached calm.

Lunch! The last thing she wanted was a polite lunch with someone she hardly knew, but she'd promised.

'I have to try to ring Kevin before I go,' she told Moira, explaining that the apricots would have to be bottled without her.

'Won't your Kevin already be on his aeroplane?'

'I hope not.' Ignoring Moira's raised eyebrows, Sophie crossed to the hall and lifted the phone again. Ten in the morning equalled about one a.m. in Belgium, she thought. If Kevin wasn't on the aeroplane then maybe she'd wake him up. The thought gave her a quite unfair sense of satisfaction.

She didn't wake him. The doubts surrounding Sophie's heart were cementing into solid certainty as Kevin's hotel answered and she asked for him. If he wasn't already on the plane. . .

'Mr Carson booked out quite some time ago,' the hotel receptionist told her. 'We believe he's flying to Australia. . .'

Mrs Lee was delighted to see Sophie. As well as someone Dr Kenrick didn't like and a fellow Englishwoman, Sophie had been present at the shooting the night before and knew everything that had happened. Sophie couldn't have been made more welcome.

As Reith had promised, Margaret Lee had roast dinner waiting—a standing rib roast beef with all the trimmings and apple pie to follow. After Moira's vast breakfast Sophie had trouble finishing, but struggled gamely. At the other end of the table Margaret Lee watched her in satisfaction, though she ate very little herself.

Conscious of the role Reith had assigned her, Sophie swung the conversation firmly in the right direction.

She might be angry with Reith Kenrick but if she was here and there really was something wrong then she could hardly do less than try.

'You served up a tiny amount to yourself, compared to what you've given me,' she pointed out. 'Margaret, I hope you're not going without to feed me.'

'Oh, I never eat very much,' the lady told her.

Sophie raised her eyebrows. 'You're trying to diet?'

Margaret gave a harsh laugh. 'I don't have to diet. I've lost so much weight. . . More apple pie, dear?'

Sophie smiled and shook her head. One more mouthful and she'd burst. 'Why have you lost weight?' she asked curiously.

'God knows.'

'Have you seen a doctor?'

The woman took a deep breath, as though fighting an inner fight—and losing.

'And have them muddling up my insides?' she said, and her voice held a quaver of fear. 'No way. If I'm dying then I intend going out my own way, without a lot of chemotherapy and radiotherapy to make me sick in the process.'

There was a long, long silence. Margaret Lee stared across the table at Sophie in horror, hearing what she'd voiced, maybe for the first time. A fear, Sophie guessed, she'd kept hidden from everyone. With a stranger, though, she'd finally let down her guard.

'You think you have cancer?' Sophie asked gently, and Margaret burst into tears.

'Oh, I shouldn't have said it. I haven't told anyone— not even my son. I've just bottled it up for so long— and I'll keep it quiet in the future for as long as I can. You won't tell anyone, will you, dear? I'm determined not to let doctors near me. I want to die with dignity.'

Sophie paused, searching for the right words. This was a fear she had seen often. The fear of dying without dignity was often a greater fear than the fear of the disease itself.

'Why do you think you have cancer?' she asked. 'If it hasn't been diagnosed. . .'

'You don't lose weight like this without there being something major wrong.' Margaret shook her head. 'The weight just seemed to drop off, even when I was eating. Now, though, it's such an effort to eat, even when I can be bothered to go shopping. I'm tired all the time—so tired. If I manage to get out to the shops then I come home and sleep. This morning I didn't get out of bed until eleven and I'm tired now.'

'That could be caused by your weight loss,' Sophie told her.

'No.' Margaret took a long drink from the glass of water before her and filled her glass again from the jug. 'I was sleepy even before I lost the weight. It's not the weight loss that caused the tiredness—it's the other way around. I can't lose much more weight without something happening—it's as if my body's being eaten away from the inside.'

'What sort of cancer do you think you have?' Sophie asked bluntly, knowing the woman would have thought it through. 'Do you have any pain?'

'Liver cancer.'

'You're very sure.'

Margaret shrugged. 'It's the only one that makes sense. I don't have any pain or discomfort and yet I'm definitely sick. It's as if it's growing down there, squeezing my bladder. I have to go to the toilet so often and I'm so thirsty. . .' She gave a frightened gasp and retreated to drink more water. 'This isn't. . .it isn't a conversation for the dinner-table.'

'I've finished my dinner,' Sophie smiled. She reached for the water jug and looked at it thoughtfully. It had been full at the start of lunch and the large jug was now close to empty. Sophie had had one small glass. She refilled her glass and emptied the jug.

'There's no growth or anything, is there, Margaret?' she asked cautiously. 'Nothing you can feel?'

'No. There's not with liver cancer. It just eats away at you, and there's nothing you can do. I've read all about it—and I'm not having chemotherapy. It makes you so sick. I want to die with my hair on.'

Sophie smiled. 'So do I,' she agreed. 'Though they make some great wigs these days. I've always fancied myself with a carrot-red beehive hairstyle.' She hesitated again, unsure how to proceed. She could take her findings back to Reith, but Margaret had asked her not to tell anyone. So. . .so she'd plug on alone. A couple more minutes of non-professional interest might pay dividends.

'Do you think you're getting worse quickly?' she asked. 'Are you sleeping more?'

'More and more.' Margaret rose to clear the table. 'I don't know how much longer I can live by myself,' she said sadly. 'I frighten myself even now.'

'Why?' Sophie stood up and started helping.

'Well. . .' The woman was still clearly reluctant to voice her fears, but to an overseas tourist she hardly knew and wasn't likely to see again it seemed safe enough. 'Well, take yesterday. I had lunch with Jenny and the baby and then I drove home. I'd just pulled into the garage when I felt all dizzy, weird. The next thing I knew it was dark and I was still sitting in the garage—four hours later.' She gave a frightened gasp. 'It was so quick. I'm not game. . .well, now I'm not game to get in the car again.'

Sophie put the plates she was carrying down on the sink and turned to Margaret. What now?

The easiest course would be to tell Reith or Jenny what she knew but then she'd betray Margaret's confidence—and she was ninety per cent sure Margaret was dangerously ill with something that could be controlled.

'That's why you're afraid of Reith Kenrick?' she said softly. 'You think he'll notice and insist on chemotherapy?'

'It's not that so much,' Margaret admitted. 'He's always been a fine doctor—and I know he'd do his best by me. It's just. . .'

'Just what?'

'Just that all these doctors, they think they're so darned clever and can cure everything, and yet when you really need them—when you have something really awful wrong with you like liver cancer—they can't do anything. I can't see a doctor now without seeing red. I know it's unfair, but it's just—why can't they cure it, Sophie?' She let the plate she was holding drop into the sink and burst into tears.

Sophie let her have her cry out. At a guess, Margaret Lee didn't give in to tears too often. She stood and waited, and finally Margaret gave a watery sniff and turned to her with the trace of a smile. A brave lady, Sophie thought.

'I'm sorry. What a dreadful lunch—'

'It was a lovely lunch.' Sophie took Margaret's hands in hers and propelled her into a chair. 'And I'm glad you've talked honestly about you, because I'm going to talk honestly about me. I'm here under false pretences.'

'False. . .?'

'I'm one of your hated doctors, Margaret. You're quite right when you say Reith Kenrick's a fine doctor. He cares about this community in a way I've seen no other doctor care. He's noted your weight loss and your fear of him, and he cares about you. He asked me to find out if there was something worrying you— something maybe we could do something about.'

Margaret was looking at Sophie in horror. 'Then you'll tell him. . .'

'No. I won't. You invited me here as a friend and if you don't want me to talk to Dr Kenrick about you then I'll respect that. But I'm going to tell you what I think. I can't be sure without doing blood-sugar tests, but I'm willing to bet my air ticket back to England that what you're suffering from is not liver cancer but diabetes. Every symptom you've described is the symptom of acute, uncontrolled diabetes mellitus. You have frequency of urine output; you seem constantly thirsty; you drift into coma and you're losing weight. Losing weight is the only symptom you have which is consistent with liver cancer, and if it was liver failure that was causing this amount of weight loss then you'd also be jaundiced. There's not a trace of yellowing about your skin.' She smiled. 'And I've been watching really, really hard.'

'But you're a doctor.'

It was a flat accusation and Sophie sighed. Had Margaret heard anything else she'd said?

'Yes.'

The silence stretched on. The big clock in the kitchen ticked with relentless rhythm while Sophie held her breath and waited.

'Diabetes, you say?'

Sophie's breath was exhaled. 'Yes.'

'But you can't be sure?'

'No. I can't be sure. But you can't be sure of liver cancer either, and I know if I was choosing between illnesses which one I'd opt for. Mature onset diabetes is usually easy to treat, often by diet alone. Once you're on treatment, your symptoms may well totally disappear, giving you a long and healthy future.'

'Diabetes. . .' Margaret was turning the suggestion over and over in her mind. 'You mean I won't be able to eat chocolate?'

Sophie grinned. 'Well, your chocolate-eating will be restricted, that's for sure. But with liver cancer there's not a lot of chocolate-eating in front of you either. I'd go for diabetes if I were you.'

Margaret sniffed, reached for her handkerchief and blew her nose. 'I've been. . . I've been stupid.'

'You've been frightened.'

She nodded. 'I guess. . .I guess I need to find out

for sure. . . That I haven't got cancer, I mean.'

'It'd be wise,' Sophie told her. 'In fact it would be sensible to do it straight away. If, as I suspect, you're falling into diabetic coma then you might injure yourself badly by losing consciousness at a worrying time. You really can't trust your body while your blood-sugar levels aren't monitored.'

'OK.' Mrs Lee took a deep breath. 'I'll need to make an appointment with Dr Kenrick, then.'

'I can take you to the surgery this afternoon if you like,' Sophie suggested. She wasn't going to push, but if Margaret was falling into coma then she really wasn't safe to leave alone. 'How about we wash these dishes and then I'll drive you down?' She didn't want the lady behind the wheel of a car until this was sorted out either.

'But he might be busy—'

'Then I'll test your sugar myself. But I think Reith Kenrick will be very pleased to see us.'

Pleased to see *you*, she should have said. After last night. . .

It won't make any difference to Reith at all, she told herself sadly. I don't affect Reith Kenrick the way he affects me. I bet he'll be courteous and scrupulously polite and he'll thank me very nicely for my help.

Toad!

Reith was courteous, scrupulously polite and thanked Sophie very nicely for her help. He was also so good with Margaret that Sophie felt her heart somersaulting all over again.

His afternoon clinic was just beginning as Sophie took Margaret in. Reith met Margaret with a smile of real friendliness and put aside her embarrassment as of no importance. He listened to Sophie's brief explanation, saw the fear in Margaret's eyes and apologised to the patients he had waiting. Margaret's fear was nerve-snapping.

Without wasting time on reassurance, Reith pricked

Margaret's finger and checked the blood sample in the glucometer immediately. The glucometer showed sugar levels of three times the normal levels and Margaret burst into tears of relief.

'I'm so stupid,' she said over and over again.

'You're not stupid,' Reith told her. 'There's nothing more worrying than your body doing things you don't understand.'

'I guess. . .' Margaret Lee looked nervously out at the patients waiting in the reception area '. . .I guess now I know I can just make an appointment for some convenient time to find out what I should do. . .'

'No.' Reith shook his head and raised his eyebrows at Sophie. 'I'm sure Dr Lynton agrees with me on this, Margaret. Diabetes is straightforward enough to control, but with blood sugars as high as yours you're likely to drift into coma at any time. There's no guarantee you won't lose consciousness while you're holding a boiling kettle or in the shower or in the time between turning on the gas and setting the flame. What I want is to admit you to hospital—now if possible. If you agree I'll get the ambulance to take you across to Lamberton and have the physician there do a thorough assessment. They'll try you on medication and adjust it until they have it right.'

'But. . .now?'

'Tell me,' Reith said gently, 'are you really confident of being by yourself at home until we have this thing controlled?'

'N-no. I guess I've been scared—'

'Well, then. . .'

'But I don't want to go in an ambulance,' Margaret declared. 'I'd feel a fraud. And my son's taking a school excursion to Melbourne today and Jenny's still worried about the baby. . .'

'I could drive you,' Sophie told her, her eyes carefully averted from Reith. She was doing anything but look at Reith. She couldn't look at the man and keep her voice steady, and the tremor in her voice was infuriating. She felt about ten years old.

'You could do that, Dr Lynton,' Reith said gravely. He was watching her, she knew, but she wouldn't meet his eyes. 'If you were to drive Margaret to Lamberton, you could solve a problem for me.'

'A problem?' She was staring at her toes.

'I sent an urgent call for help to Lamberton last night. They had a road smash on their hands and could send only an ambulance car with one officer. When the helicopter arrived it had a doctor on board but no paramedic, so the ambulance officer went in the helicopter to assist. The ambulance is therefore still here.'

'So you want me to drive it back to Lamberton?'

'It'd save someone a job—and with one of their officers still in Melbourne Lamberton are short-staffed.'

'How would I get back?'

'There's the neat part,' Reith told her. 'I have a very old lady in the hospital in Lamberton who I badly want to see. She's dying and her daughter sent a message that she wants to talk to me. I thought I'd drive over after clinic—so I could bring you back. I'd take Margaret over then, but to be honest, Sophie, with a blood sugar as high as she has, the sooner she's in hospital the happier I'll be. She's a walking time bomb. This arrangement seems to suit us all.'

'Very neat,' Sophie said waspishly. She ventured a look at Reith, and to her fury found that the look on his face was one of amusement.

'But I won't go in an ambulance,' Margaret announced.

'Not even sitting up the front supervising Dr Lynton's performance on Australian roads?' Reith queried. 'She hasn't done too well so far. She's a danger to our wildlife if ever I met one.' The laughter in his voice made Sophie's teeth clench.

'I don't know. . .' Margaret hesitated.

'It is sensible,' Sophie conceded, looking at Margaret rather than those mocking eyes. There was another factor in Reith's suggesting the ambulance as a mode of transport, she knew. It would be equipped with what she needed if Margaret collapsed in a full hyper. 'I'll take you home on the way and collect your night things—and you'll let them know at Lamberton that we're coming?' How to ask Reith a question and not look at him?

'I'll let them know. And Sophie. . .' he put a hand out and touched her lightly on the cheek '. . .I do appreciate it.'

I'll bet, thought Sophie.

The journey across to Lamberton was uneventful. Margaret dozed beside her all the way, never far from sleep with her blood sugars so elevated, and Sophie was left to her own reflections.

They weren't very peaceful. Her mind was a jumble of Kevin and Reith in some crazy kaleidoscopic pattern, whirling around her mind in an agony of indecision.

How could she marry Kevin when she had discovered how she really could feel about a man? How could she marry Kevin when Reith was superimposed on everything she did? It was even impossible to summon the image of Kevin's face in her head, as Reith was there already, those dark, mocking eyes haunted with the scars of solitude. . .

With Margaret safely settled into hospital, treatment started and her blood sugars being monitored carefully, Sophie was free to explore the country town of Lamberton.

It was a town that lived off the sheep's back. . .rural, easygoing, and about twenty or thirty years behind the times, Sophie thought, and found she didn't mind a bit. What would it be like living in a place where this was the major shopping centre?

She walked slowly along the street, looking at shops selling such things as sheep dip and dog collars, and garages that sold combine harvesters and tractors. It was about as far as she could get from London, England. A whole new world. . .

She bought scones and jam and cream from a stall set up by the Country Women's Association and then wandered down by the river to eat them. Her sense of unreality was deepening by the moment. How could she calmly go back to practise medicine in England after this? Her heart was here, and she had a feeling that, no matter where her body went from this day forth, her heart would stay very firmly in this place.

Reith was due at the hospital at seven. Half an hour for him to do what he had to—speak to a woman who was dying. No kudos for him in that! No reason for him to make the sixty-mile round trip.

Damn the man. She was so in love with him that it was twisting her in knots. She couldn't think about him dispassionately.

Other doctors cared for their patients. Other doctors were skilled and devoted and. . .

That line of thinking didn't work. There was only one Reith Kenrick. He had burned himself into her heart and he was there to stay. Somehow she had to organise the rest of her life around that.

So what to do? Tell Reith he was loved? Throw herself at him?

That was the action of a fool. It didn't take many brains to know that such an action was the one thing designed to make a man run so fast that you couldn't see him for dust. Reith Kenrick had declared he wanted no one, and there was nothing Sophie could do to change that.

She was sitting on the dry-grassed river bank, idly throwing pebbles out into the still water. The ripples moved further and further out, changing the calm surface into a whirling sketch-pad of rings. One stone and the surface of the whole river changed. One man. . .

He didn't want her. Sophie's place was not here. It was back in London—with Kevin.

No!

She stood, looking out at the water, and her mind firmed into at least one resolution. She didn't need Kevin's odd form of security. She had moved past it. She could maybe make a life for herself on her own, feeling as she did about Reith, but that life couldn't include Kevin. It would be a mockery and a sham.

But Kevin's coming, she thought.

'It can't be helped,' she said to herself ruefully. 'He'll just have to go home again. We'll both have to go home.'

Home. Why did the word sound so bleak? It was because somehow home no longer seemed London's bustling metropolis and fog-bound skies. Home was hot and dusty and smelled of eucalypts and sheep droppings and—

'Get a grip on yourself, Sophie Lynton,' she told herself harshly. 'Get yourself together. You have to drive back to Inyabarra tonight with Reith Kenrick. You're going to have to be formally polite and distant, and then you're going to have to leave this place as fast as possible—before Reith Kenrick destroys what's left of your precious sanity.'

CHAPTER EIGHT

REITH was waiting for Sophie at seven-thirty when she made her way back to the hospital. He was leafing through journals in the reception area and stood abruptly as she entered.

'I'm sorry,' Sophie faltered, glancing at her watch. 'You said seven-thirty. Have I kept you waiting?'

He shook his head, weariness lurking in his eyes. 'No. My appointment here took less time than I'd anticipated.'

'A problem?' She guessed there was by his look of defeat.

'Yeah.' He dug his hands into his pockets. 'Blasted relatives. Do you want to go out to dinner?'

The question took her by surprise. Reith was neatly dressed in sports trousers and short-sleeved business shirt, but Sophie looked down at her casual frock with doubt. Her toes were bare in soft sandals and her hair hung free and tousled from the wind by the river.

'I'm not suggesting we go formal,' Reith said, guessing her concern. 'Friends of mine run a small restaurant north of here on the river. Thursday night's quiet.'

The doubt wasn't only because of her clothes. Sophie looked up at Reith and winced inside. She should refuse. She should. . .

There was little she could refuse this man. Love and good sense seemed as incompatible as chalk and cheese.

'I'd like that,' she said simply.

Reith hadn't deceived her when he had said the place was informal. The Pink Cockatoo was a tiny restaurant capable of seating only about twenty. On this balmy summer night the tables were set out under gum trees,

112

the river running deep and cool twenty feet from the restaurant's huge French windows. Around them, searching fallen gum nuts for seed, were the birds that gave the restaurant its name.

'The restaurant floods most winters,' Reith told her, seeing Sophie's look of amazement at how close the water ran. 'But Liz and Tony reckon it's worth cleaning out the mud for a view like this.'

Liz and Tony, a couple in their mid-sixties but with the bounce of a couple of teenagers, met Reith with the delight of old friends. Sophie was welcomed with warmth—and curiosity only just held in check.

'It's a quiet night,' Tony beamed, his eyes taking in Sophie's appearance with an appreciation that made Sophie blush. 'Not good for business but great for you two. Where shall we put them, Mother?'

He settled them outside, filled their glasses with ice-cold moselle and bustled off to see to their order.

'You come here often?' Sophie asked, searching for a way to break the ice. Having asked her to dinner, Reith obviously saw no need for polite chat. He sat back in his chair and looked out over the river, his face reflecting weariness.

'Yes.' With an effort Reith dragged his attention back to her. 'I shouldn't. It's a fair way from Inyabarra if things go wrong. Still. . .' he motioned to his mobile phone '. . .I can get there fast enough if I'm called and sometimes. . .sometimes being on call for twenty-four hours a day takes its toll.'

'Like now,' Sophie said gently, seeing the exhaustion settle over his face. 'You had little enough sleep last night. You should be home in your bed right now.'

'I wouldn't sleep,' he said bluntly. The weariness faded a little and his eyes flashed dangerous humour. 'Though if I had someone in my bed to take my mind off things. . .'

'Buy yourself a bedside radio,' Sophie managed. Her face flushed crimson. Drat the man. . .

'OK.' Reith smiled and spread his hands in mock apology. 'Enough. I should be grateful that you've agreed to have dinner with me.'

The man really was lonely. Solitude was all very well, Sophie thought with a flash of insight, but not being able to talk over medical problems must be the pits. When things went wrong professionally it was almost essential for her that she debrief herself—talk over what happened with colleagues until at least she could see the thing with clear perspective.

'So what went wrong tonight?' she asked. 'What happened to make Dr Kenrick need company for an hour or two?'

His eyebrows lifted in surprise. 'Is it so obvious— that I'm using you as debriefing?'

Their minds worked on the same channel. 'Yes. It's obvious.'

Reith picked up his wine glass, running one long, lean finger round and round the rim.

'Nothing went wrong. Medicine saved a life. It's just. . .well, that life didn't particularly want to be saved.'

'Meaning?'

He sighed. 'I have a very old and very gentle lady in hospital, dying of emphysema. At the weekend she suffered a cardiac arrest. May's ninety-three, she's been in hospital for months and she wants to die. Actively. Her husband died six months ago. She has cardiac failure, her legs won't hold her up any more, she has ulcers which, if she lives much longer, are going to lead to gangrene and amputation, and she's miserably lonely. So, when her heart gave out on Sunday, it was a kindness.'

'But she didn't die.'

'No. She wasn't permitted. Her niece was in the hospital when May arrested. The niece screamed blue murder until the crash cart arrived, threatened legal action all around unless the doctor on duty tried everything—so the young doctor pulled out all stops and resuscitated. They got May back without any brain damage. Now, though, May's anything but grateful. She asked me to make sure it doesn't happen next time. She wants to be allowed to go.'

'And isn't that possible?'

'It should be,' Reith agreed. 'When patients are as terminally ill as May is they can request and receive a standing order, "Not For Resuscitation". May already has that order written on her chart, placed there at her request. Her niece, though. . . Well, her niece stands to inherit May's considerable fortune and thinks the more fuss she makes at this stage the more she'll deserve the old lady's money. She's hardly visited May until the last couple of weeks, when it was clear the end was near. She's now threatening the hospital with lawsuits if they don't do everything to extend the old lady's life. In her eyes it justifies her inheritance.'

'So?'

'So.' Reith put the glass flatly on the table. 'So I had to contact a lawyer and get a statement drawn up in front of witnesses that the "Not For Resuscitation" order stands, and both aunt and niece are dreadfully upset. . .' Reith shook his head. 'The last thing May needs is conflict. I wish I'd been there on Sunday.'

'But you don't want to be a hospital doctor,' Sophie said gently.

'No. Though I've sometimes thought. . .'

'Thought what?'

'If another doctor could be persuaded to come to Inyabarra we could set up a four-bed clinic—just for people like May who don't want to leave the town to die. It could be useful for emergency theatre too. But. . .'

'But Inyabarra's not big enough to support another doctor.'

Reith gave a rueful smile. 'There wouldn't be enough money for luxuries, that's for sure. How about you,

Dr Lynton? Would you be prepared to walk away from your well-paying city practice and move here? Be on call twenty-four hours a day? No highways; no bitumen; no specialists on call; no other doctors to talk to and no private schools for your kids?'

'Is that an invitation?' Sophie licked suddenly dry lips.

'You reckon you could persuade the convenient Kevin to move here, do you, Dr Lynton? It's a far cry from business trips to Belgium.'

'No,' Sophie said slowly. 'Kevin wouldn't come. But. . .but I might be persuaded to stay.'

'What, without Kevin?' Reith was startled.

'Maybe.'

'You're air dreaming, Dr Lynton,' Reith said brutally. 'Dreaming the classic dream of all holidaymakers. What if. . . What if I stayed here and made this my life? You've left your worries behind in London. You're minus the responsibility of even a boyfriend and it feels good. So. . .'

'So I make an offer I have no intention of honouring?' Sophie nodded, her eyes bleak. 'You may be right.'

'It was a very generous offer,' Reith said gently and Sophie's head flew up.

'Don't patronise me, Dr Kenrick,' she snapped.

'I'm not patronising—'

'Laughing, then!'

'Yes,' he said solemnly. 'I'm amused that you think you could stick this place. Plenty of stronger women than you have tried and failed.'

'Like your mother.'

'Like my mother,' he agreed and then dropped the conversation like a hot brick as his meal arrived.

Sophie had ordered at Reith's direction. 'Don't touch the kangaroo or the crocodile,' he directed. 'The tourists demand it, so it has to be on the menu, but our ancestors knew what they were about when they imported cows, sheep and pigs. The local treat here, though, is the yabbies, and you should try them.'

'Yabbies?'

'A cross between prawns and lobsters, but they come straight from fresh-water mud.'

'They sound disgusting.'

'They're not. Try and see, Dr Lynton.'

She could refuse him nothing. . .

The yabbies arrived in a glistening, steaming broth, tender red crustaceans in a concoction of wine and herbs that made Sophie's mouth water. The over-powering roast lunch Margaret had served seemed a long time away. She tackled the tender meat with relish, and was amazed to find herself coming back for a third helping of the warm, home-baked bread.

'This place does that to you,' Reith told her when she commented that she hadn't expected to be hungry. 'Real home-baked cooking. . . It's the only place I can get it.'

Sophie raised her eyebrows sardonically. 'Really, Dr Kenrick? I would have thought there would have been mobs of district ladies offering home-cooked meals just for you.'

'Yeah,' Reith said drily. 'Home-cooked meals come with strings. Mortgages and garbage on Monday nights and nappies and parent-teacher interviews. . .'

'Well, isn't it lucky that I can't cook, then?' Sophie told him. 'No threat, Dr Kenrick.'

It silenced him.

There was little conversation through the rest of the meal. Liz and Tony bustled around, producing mouth-watering orange and raspberry tart with clotted cream, followed by brewed coffee, chocolate and cheese. Their hosts kept a wary eye on them, as though wondering what on earth was going on.

Nothing was going on, Sophie thought bleakly. Nothing would.

They drove home in silence, through the farmland

and into the bush of the National Park. Even if they had wanted to talk, it wasn't possible over the roar of Reith's engine.

'For heaven's sake,' Sophie yelled once above the noise. 'Why don't you get yourself a decent car?'

'Kevin drives a Mercedes, does he?' Reith enquired politely and Sophie almost gnashed her teeth. Kevin did.

Soon they were twisting into the mountains on the roads where Sophie had become so hopelessly lost a few days before. So much had changed since then.

Sophie ventured a look sideways at Reith's grim profile. Things might have changed for Sophie, but nothing had changed for Reith Kenrick.

'Know where you are?' Reith asked, intercepting her look.

'N-no.'

'This is just about where our friend koala nearly came to grief the other night.'

He rounded the bend, jammed his foot on the brake and swore. Sitting bang in the centre of the road was one small koala.

Sophie stared down at the little grey creature in astonishment. 'Is it. . .? Surely it can't be the same one?'

'An individual who likes living dangerously.' Reith steered the truck to the side of the road and parked. 'Want to try your luck at moving koalas again, Dr Lynton?'

'No.'

He grinned. 'You'll leave it to us masochistic males. Not a particularly feminist attitude!'

Sophie climbed out of the cab as Reith crossed to the koala, glad, if truth be known, to ease her body after the bone-jolting journey. She stood and watched in the moonlight as Reith expertly lifted the koala, held him in the truck lights and examined him.

'Is he hurt?'

'No. Do you fancy a walk or will you be all right to stay with the truck for a bit?'

'Why?' Sophie was startled.

'Because this animal is exactly the same one you nearly hit the other night. See the scar running down from his eye—and that patch of fur missing from his leg? He's obviously got himself a penchant for sitting on roadways. It's my guess he's carrying a few fleas and the gravel makes a nice spot to scratch his backside.'

Sophie choked on a gurgle of laughter, entranced. 'You're kidding.'

'Would I joke about something so important?' Reith smiled. 'Problem is, now he's in the habit, if he stays here he's going to get himself killed. The only thing to do is cart him a few hundred yards into thick bush where he won't be able to locate the road until he forgets how nice it is for bottom-scratching. Coming, Dr Lynton?'

'What, now?'

'What better time?'

'But. . .' Sophie looked nervously about her. 'Won't we get lost?'

'If you don't want to come, then stay here,' Reith said carelessly and strode off into the bush.

Sophie cast a nervous glance back at the truck. To stay here by herself in the bush. . .

Something behind her gave a roar like a stuck pig and she fled into the bush after Reith as if there were an electric prod at her back.

Reith was laughing when she caught up with him. The gums were huge, stretching high toward the moonlight, making it clear underfoot and easy to see a moving shadow in the darkness. That was all Reith was—a large, purposeful figure, koala held easily out in front. The koala's claws had stopped slashing—the koala obviously resigning itself to whatever fate was in store.

'Not feeling very brave, Dr Lynton?' Having caught up, Sophie was sticking close.

'It's not that. It's just—' The frightful roar broke the stillness of the night once again and it was all Sophie could do not to clutch Reith's arm. 'What on earth is that noise?'

'A koala.'

'I beg your pardon?' Sophie gazed blankly across at Reith and stumbled on a fallen branch. 'Koalas don't make a noise like that.'

'They don't in souvenir shops,' Reith agreed, waiting patiently as she regained her footing. 'I guess I wouldn't either if I was stuffed. The chap out there is declaring himself to the ladies of the district. It's romance you hear in the air, Dr Lynton.'

Sophie swallowed. 'How. . .how sweet.'

Reith chuckled. 'How are your feet?' He looked down at her sandals. 'Not really dressed for bush hiking, Dr Lynton. I'd sing as I walked if I were you.'

'Sing. . .'

'To ward off the odd Joe Blake.'

Sophie was losing it. 'J. . . Joe Blake?'

'Joe Blake. Australian for snake. They're a bit thick on the ground around here.'

Sophie uttered a yelp of distress and stopped moving. All of a sudden London was looking good.

'I thought you liked this place.' Reith smiled. He paused once again and turned round, his sardonic eyes glinting in unholy amusement in the moonlight. 'Am I putting you off, Dr Lynton?'

'Are there really snakes?'

'There really are snakes.' Reith relented then, seeing her real look of fear, adding, 'I wouldn't worry, though. I wouldn't have asked you to come into the bush if I was concerned. They're cold-blooded creatures and are mostly only active in the daytime. At this time of night they should be safely curled up digesting all the delicious little ground creatures they poisoned today.'

'Ugh.'

'Want to go home, Dr Lynton?'

'Yes!' The sooner the better for her sanity.

Finally, thankfully, Reith deemed they had travelled far enough from the road. He released the koala onto the trunk of a towering eucalypt. Without a backward glance, the koala headed for the heavens.

'You'd think he'd stop and say thank you.' Reith grinned.

'You probably separated him from his girlfriends.'

'Maybe I did at that,' Reith agreed. 'If so, then maybe I've done him a second favour.'

'As far as I know,' Sophie said drily, 'koalas don't have garbage nights, nappies or parent-teacher interviews.'

'Maybe they do have emotional dependence, though,' Reith told her. He turned back toward the road. 'Coming, Dr Lynton?' His hands free, he reached out and caught hers, leading her forward into the night.

'There's no need to hold my hand.' Sophie tugged to be released but his grip tightened.

'I don't want to lose you.'

'Ha!' She said it before thinking.

'Sophie. . .'

'What?' She snapped the word crossly, angry with herself for letting emotion show. Still he held her hand, and his grip was warm and reassuring in the loneliness of the night. If only it could go on. . .

'I should never have kissed you,' Reith said harshly. 'For heaven's sake, woman, it was a kiss—not a declaration of intent.'

'For you maybe. . .' She shouldn't say it but to have him think otherwise would be a lie.

'Sophie, this is stupid.'

'Yes, it is, isn't it?' she managed. 'I'm a happily engaged girl and you're a man who wants no one. So this feeling between us is stupid and senseless and pointless and. . .and will you let my hand go?'

'You won't fall?'

'I won't fall without you, Reith Kenrick.'

Brave words. If only she could be sure they were true.

It was almost eleven by the time they reached Sophie's guest house. To Sophie's surprise, the lights were all still on and Moira came hurrying out onto the veranda to meet them.

'Oh, Sophie,' she said anxiously, 'I was hoping you'd come soon. The wee one has been sobbing and sobbing—I can't get her to sleep.'

Sophie closed her eyes in distress. She had promised to stay. . .'I shouldn't have gone to Lamberton.'

'Of course you should have,' Moira told her roundly. 'Dr Kenrick needed you.' It was a reason that overrode everything with Moira, Sophie realised—Dr Kenrick's need. . .

'I'll come.' Sophie scrambled out of the truck, aware that Reith too was climbing out. 'There's no need for you—'

'Mandy's my patient.' Reith took the veranda steps two at a time beside Sophie.

Mandy was past reason. She had been sobbing for hours, the blind, unreasoning sobbing of a child frightened past logic. The wails were weak with fatigue and the tiny shoulders heaved with desperate abandon. Mandy was bereft of everything, and the night had brought the weight of a vast and frightening world down upon her.

'Mandy. . .' Sophie knelt to gather the child to her, but Mandy would have none of it. She held her little body rigid with distress.

'She's been like this since dark,' Moira told them. 'I didn't know what to do. I darn near called you, Dr Kenrick.'

'You should have,' Reith said briefly. 'I was carrying the phone. We could have been back three hours ago.'

'Well, I didn't want to disturb you,' Moira told him, with a sideways glance at Sophie that had her wondering just how much the lady guessed of what Sophie was feeling. 'And she's not sick.'

'She will be if she keeps this up.' Reith lifted Mandy's rigid body up from Sophie's arms and carried her outside. Wondering, Sophie and Moira followed.

The coolness of the night breeze hit Mandy's flushed, swollen face like cool water. It caught at the child's consciousness, penetrating her misery enough to let her pause for breath. Reith took immediate advantage.

'I want no more noise, Mandy Bell.'

The child's chin wobbled. Tears slid down the woebegone face and her lip quivered in readiness of further crying.

'I mean that,' Reith growled. 'I'm walking down the stairs out into the garden right now, and it's dark. You'd better keep very quiet and still and let me concentrate or you'll have us both upside-down in Mrs Sanderson's prickle bush.'

There was enough of the unknown in what was happening for Reith to gain the child's full attention. Mandy glanced fearfully, uncertainly up at Reith's face and stayed silent.

'Now,' Reith told her, 'no more noise, my Mandy, and I'll tell you what's going to happen. Listening?'

There was the merest quiver of agreement in the rigid body.

'Right.' Agreement was assumed. 'Mrs Sanderson is going to bed. Right now,' Reith growled, at Moira's quick shake of her head. 'The lady was up half last night and is exhausted and she's been getting more and more tired trying to stop you crying, Miss Mandy. You want Mrs Sanderson to look after you until Mary gets back, don't you, Mandy? If you do, then she goes to bed now.'

He cast a stern, directing glare at Moira, who opened her mouth to protest, thought better of it and retired from the lists.

'Next,' Reith told the child in his arms, 'Dr Sophie and I are going to sit on the big log swing with you until you go to sleep. But if you start crying again it's going to be very, very uncomfortable for all of us, so I want you to stay quiet. Can you do that, Mandy?'

'Y. . .yes.' It was a terrified quiver and Sophie's heart wrenched inside her.

'We're not going to leave you, Mandy. That's a promise. There will always be someone here with you, wherever you are, asleep or awake. Soon it will be Mary and Ted, but for now it will be Mrs Sanderson, Dr Sophie or me. Right. We're going to swing and swing and swing until your little eyes finally close, and after you go to sleep we're going to tuck you into bed beside Dr Sophie and let you sleep until morning. When you wake up, Dr Sophie will be here, and Mrs Sanderson—people who love and care for you until your Mary and Ted can come back from Melbourne and tuck you home in their little house. Any questions?'

It seemed there weren't.

The rigid little body stayed rigid, but the wails had ceased. Mandy, it seemed, was giving them the benefit of the doubt.

'Right, Dr Sophie. . .' Reith strode across the garden to where a big log swing hung on the branches of an overhanging gum and organised his long body on the swing. There was just enough room for two. 'Come and swing with us.'

'I'll watch.'

'Dr Sophie. . .' He growled.

'Y. . . Yes?'

'Come here and sit!'

She sat.

It was half an hour before Mandy finally slept, and

by the time she did Sophie was near to sleep herself. The warm night breeze enfolded them. Around the swing were flowering gums, and the blossoms—soft white cloud-bursts of scented honey—were intoxicating in their beauty. Sophie looked down at the sleeping child in Reith's arms and found herself inexplicably near to tears.

'I'll take her in now,' she said, and her voice was unsteady.

'Give her a moment. Wait until she's so soundly asleep that we won't risk waking her.'

Sophie nodded. 'Poor little mite.'

'She'll survive,' Reith told her. 'She'll have love and security with Mary and Ted, and turn out nicely normal and go on to a nice secure fiancé and brick veneer and kids—'

'There's nothing wrong with that,' Sophie retorted, hearing the note of derision in his voice.

'That's what you're doing, isn't it, Sophie? Looking for the next round of security. In Kevin.'

The next round. . . There had never been a first round.

A lump as big as a fist was wedged hard in Sophie's throat. This man knew nothing of her, and cared even less. He would never find out what was behind Sophie's need.

'She's fast asleep,' Sophie said abruptly and heard the tears in her voice. She stood up, making the swing rock as she rose. 'Give her to me.'

'I'll carry her in.'

'N-no.' She didn't want this man in her bedroom any more. She couldn't let herself anywhere near him.

'Sophie. . .' Reith had also risen. He stood in the moonlight, the sleeping child in his arms, and stood looking down at Sophie. His mobile eyebrows drew together, as if the great Reith Kenrick, for once, was off balance. 'What's happened between us is holiday madness,' he said gently and Sophie winced.

'Yes.' Say anything, she told herself. Just get away from here.

'You know you could never be happy here.'

She took a deep breath. 'So you say. And you're never wrong, Reith Kenrick. You judge people by your own criteria and you never open yourself to doubt. Look, just give me Mandy and just go home.'

Go home. . . A bleak command. It hung between them in its bleakness and the uncertainty stayed on Reith's face. As if, for one moment, he was unsure.

'Kevin's coming tomorrow?'

'Yes. No. I. . .I think so.'

Reith nodded. 'Well, there you are, then, Sophie. Your "happy ever after" is about to begin.'

'Kevin's not my "happy ever after".'

'He's your fiancé, Sophie. Your future.'

'No.'

The word stretched out in the stillness of the night, intense and forlorn. Why was she still standing here—fighting for something she had no hope of ever achieving?

It was almost a relief to turn away at the sound of a car, to look away from Reith's dark eyes and stare out along the track at the approaching vehicle. It seemed that Reith also welcomed the intrusion. They stood side by side and waited while the coming car slowed, turned into the guest house driveway and drew to a halt.

Sophie knew even before the car door opened who it was. It was a hire-car, but an expensive one, with the hire firm's logo discreetly shown on the Mercedes' rear window.

A Mercedes. . .

Kevin.

CHAPTER NINE

KEVIN stood uncertainly in the driveway, staring up at
the house as if unsure he had come to the right place.
From where he stood he couldn't know that he was
being watched.

Sophie's fiancé was as immaculate as ever, the
impeccable cut of his Italian suit obvious even in the
dim light. It would take more than a two-day inter-
national flight to ruffle Kevin's grooming.

It didn't affect Sophie one bit. Usually Sophie felt
a rush of gratitude and pleasure at the sight of Kevin—
a gratitude that had grown as a lonely teenager when
Kevin had first taken her under his wing. Now it was
a real effort to move forward.

Reith was the first to speak.

'Dr Lynton,' Reith said drily down to Sophie, 'if this
is your errant boyfriend, I dare say he's expecting a
welcome. May I suggest you go say hello?'

To her fury, Sophie heard laughter in Reith's voice.
Drat the man. . .

'Kevin!' She called out and forced herself to take a
step forward.

'Sophia. . .' There was relief in Kevin's tone as he
turned. He took two steps in Sophie's direction and
then stopped in astonishment as his eyes became accustomed to the dark. Finally he took in the scenario of
couple and child. 'Sophia?'

'Sophia?' Reith quizzed softly, the laughter inten-
sifying. 'Well, I never. I've never known a real Sophia
before.'

Sophie swallowed and stepped into Kevin's abrupt
embrace. The embrace was perfunctory. She was
released in seconds and Kevin stared at Reith, waiting

127

for introductions. Somehow she forced herself to make them.

'Kevin, this is Dr Reith Kenrick. Reith. . . Kevin Carson.'

'What the. . .?' There was no way Kevin could shake Reith's hand even if he'd wanted to. Reith's arms were fully occupied with the sleeping child. 'What the hell is going on, Sophia?'

'We. . .' Sophie was right off balance and it showed. 'Reith. . . Dr Kenrick is the local doctor. Mandy. . . this little girl's father is. . .is ill and we're looking after her.'

'Both of you? In the garden at midnight?' Kevin sounded incredulous, and Sophie could see his point.

'No. Mrs Sanderson. . .the owner of the guest house. . .and I have been looking after Mandy. I. . . Dr Kenrick and I have been busy this afternoon with another patient. We got home late and Mandy was upset. . .' Her voice trailed to nothing. To her fury she felt like a child caught out in wrongdoing.

'You mean you've been working?' Kevin was clearly at a loss, and reacted as he always did when things weren't going to his liking—with anger. 'Medically? Sophia, you're here on holiday.'

'On her honeymoon, I hear,' Reith said helpfully and gave Sophie a bland smile. 'You've been working in Belgium, I gather, and Dr Lynton's been working in Inyabarra. Strange honeymoon—but each to his own. Shall I put Mandy in your bedroom—Sophia?'

It was as much as Sophie could do not to grind her teeth out loud. 'Yes, thank you, Dr Kenrick. I'll come in with you—'

'There's no need.' His smile was still as bland as cream. Reith Kenrick was enjoying himself and it showed. 'I should know the way to your bedroom by now. You stay here and welcome your fiancé properly.' He smiled across to Kevin. 'Welcome to Australia, Kevin. I'm pleased for Sophia that you finally showed.'

He turned back to Sophie and the mockery faded for an instant. 'Maybe I won't see you again, Dr Lynton. Accept my best wishes for your future happiness.'

And for a trace, a fleeting particle of a second, Sophie saw a flicker of regret in his eyes.

And then he was gone.

Sophie hadn't realised how restful Moira Sanderson's guest house had been until Kevin's arrival. The rest stopped with Kevin.

By the time Sophie fell into bed she was exhausted. Kevin was incredulous, angry and belligerent.

First there had been demands to explain Reith Kenrick—and Sophie had done her best. Her explanation had left Kevin disgruntled.

Moira had come out then to find out who the strange voice belonged to—and her next statement had taken Kevin's breath away.

'I've prepared a downstairs bedroom for you,' she told him severely.

'But. . .' Kevin's eyes snapped annoyance. 'Sophia has a double room. There's no problem.'

'As long as you don't mind sleeping with the door open into Mandy's room,' Sophie said doubtfully, her heart sinking at the thought of Kevin in her room. She'd have to share Mandy's bed. She couldn't sleep with Kevin—but neither could she tell him that here, in front of Moira.

'I do, as a matter of fact,' Kevin snapped. 'But we can talk about that in private.' Moira's bobbing curlers were clearly not what he was used to in hotel staff. 'I'll take my luggage up now.' He would have preferred a porter, his tone said.

'No.' Moira's arms folded across her crimson-robed bosom and she stood before the stairway as though defending the honour of her house. 'The girls sleep upstairs. Men downstairs, if you don't mind, Mr Carson.'

'We booked a double room,' Kevin said silkily.

'You booked as a married couple.' The arms stayed folded and Sophie suppressed the unchristian thought that, like Reith, Moira was enjoying herself. 'Dr Lynton herself told me you're not yet married and while you're under my roof there's no hanky-panky between unwed children.'

'I'm hardly a child,' Kevin snapped between thinned lips. 'And neither is Sophia.'

'You're a child compared to me, and Sophie Lynton's an unwed girl with no mother to protect her. I know my duty. This is a decent house and I intend to keep it that way. If you want to move out then it's fine by me. There's motels in Lamberton.'

Kevin practically gaped. He glared from Sophie to Moira and back to Sophie.

Then he held out his hand to Sophie in an imperative gesture of command.

'Collect your things, Sophia. We needn't put up with this nonsense.'

Sophie swallowed. 'I can't leave, Kevin,' she said gently. 'Mandy. . .I promised Mandy I'd stay until. . . until she can go home.'

'Mandy?'

'The little girl.'

His eyes widened. 'And how long do you think that will be?'

'I don't know.'

They stood in the dim hall light, with Sophie feeling more miserable than she had ever felt in her life. She wished the floor would open up and swallow her. Heaven, she needed time to sort herself out.

Around her heart, though, was a penetrating mist of gratitude for Moira's stand. Moira had given her the breathing space she so badly needed.

'This child's not your patient,' Kevin snapped finally. 'It's not your place—'

'It is my place,' Sophie said softly. 'It is.'

She lay in her big bed alone now, and spent the night staring at patterns on the ceiling, seeing anything but. What on earth was she to do? What?

The next day brought no answers. Kevin was rigid with fury, but his mobile phone and portable fax kept him occupied for most of the morning. Sophie's suggestion that she take him sightseeing was met with blank incomprehension.

'See what, Sophia?'

'The land around here,' Sophie said miserably. 'The mountains. Maybe. . .maybe I might even find you a koala. I know where to look.'

'You go,' he said uninterestedly. 'I have to finish this.'

Sophie stared at him for a long moment. 'Kevin,' she said at last, 'why did you come?'

He looked up at that. His eyes creased into the smile she'd known for so long—the smile that had reassured her as an insecure teenager that here was someone who would take the worries of the world onto his shoulders—and be her rock. They'd been each other's security for so long. . . A habit it was time to break.

'I came because you were here,' he said simply. 'You know I always do.'

'Eventually.'

'Sophia, I'm a busy man,' he explained patiently. 'You understand that.'

'Who was the woman in Belgium?'

'Who?'

'The woman with you when you called me.'

'There was no woman.'

It was said too fast. There was no time behind his response for thought about where he had made the phone call or who had been with him—just a harsh, flat denial that had the opposite effect to reassurance on Sophie. His snapped denial said he had been ready for the question. It was a confirmation of what she had expected.

'How long,' she said carefully, 'do you think we might stay here?'

'You've already told me—until the kid is claimed. Though why the hell you had to make promises. . . It's lucky I've got the fax and computer with me.'

'And then?'

'We'll go home, of course.'

'And the wedding?'

'We'll have it some-time, sweetheart.' He grinned and bent again over his laptop computer. 'After all, Sophia, we've known each other long enough. It doesn't really matter if we're married or not.'

'No.'

He didn't hear the dreary inflexion in her voice. She opened her mouth to say more but the mobile telephone rang, the fax vibrated into use with an incoming message and Kevin waved her away with his hand. Interview suspended.

So now what? Frustrated from the confrontation she'd intended, Sophie wandered outside and sat on the log swing she'd used the night before with Reith, swinging it gently back and forth as her mind came to grips with her future. A future without Kevin. And a future without Reith. . .

'Sophie.'

Sophie looked up. Moira was waving a tea-towel from the back door.

'Sophie, you're wanted on the telephone.'

Who on earth. . .? There was a tiny flicker of hope, quickly suppressed. Moira's next words doused the hope completely.

'It's Elvira Pilkington, Sophie—the woman who had hysterics the night Mandy's dad died. I don't know what she wants with you but she's demanding to speak to the lady doctor and it's a wonder you can't hear her yelling from here.'

Moira wasn't exaggerating. Sophie picked up the receiver and the woman's shrill tone made her wince and hold the phone at arm's length.

'Dr Lynton. . . Dr Lynton. . .I want you to come straight away. Something awful is wrong with my daughter. My lovely Christabelle. . . She's locked herself in her room and she's crying and crying and when she walked into the house she looked like death and she vomited in the downstairs toilet but she wouldn't let me come near her and now she's gone all quiet and she won't let me in and I. . .I'm scared. I've been yelling at her to come out for an hour but she hasn't talked except when I said I'd get Dr Kenrick and then she yelled that if any man came near her she'd die— she'd just die—and Dr Lynton. . .I think she means it—'

The woman's voice cracked on a noisy sob and there was a sudden blessed silence. There was time for Sophie to think.

'Isn't Christabelle Dr Kenrick's patient?' she asked gently and held the receiver out again.

'I tried to ring him,' Elvira told her, 'but Christabelle's got a phone extension in her room and she said she'd kill herself if I so much as rang him.'

Elvira's voice had quietened a little. The distinct wobble to her words made Sophie suspect that, despite her hysterical personality, the woman really was badly frightened.

'What if I rang him?' Sophie suggested, thinking fast. Reith was much more likely to know what was troubling the girl than she was.

There was a frantic gasp on the other end of the line and a tight, terrified voice cut in. Christabelle, it seemed, was still listening.

'No! No! I don't want a man. Oh, God, I'll die. . . Mum, don't you dare let her ring him. No! I'll kill myself. . .'

The voice ended on an hysterical wail and Sophie

took a deep breath. There was enough real terror in the voice to make Sophie take the girl's threat seriously. Hysterical teenage girls could be capable of anything.

'I'll come over and talk to you, Christabelle,' she said softly, and then winced as the mother's voice yelled down the line again.

'Oh, would you, Dr Lynton? A real lady doctor? You hear that, Christabelle? Dr Lynton's coming now. You'll be right. . .'

'I'll be there in five minutes,' Sophie said firmly and replaced the yelling receiver.

She stood in thought for thirty seconds, Moira watching from a distance. Mandy came through from the kitchen, her small face coated in chocolate-cake mix, and the two waited for Sophie to come to a decision.

'I'll go,' Sophie said finally. 'They really were frightened, weren't they, Moira?'

'They were,' Moira agreed. 'Otherwise I wouldn't have agreed to call you to the telephone.'

'How old is Christabelle?'

'Fourteen. And boy mad already.'

'Can you tell me how to get there?'

'Sure.'

'Are you going away?' Mandy asked solemnly. She took another lick of her wooden spoon and regarded it thoughtfully. 'Mrs Sanderson and me don't want you to go, but him. . .' She gestured with her spoon to Kevin's intent figure in the dining-room. 'He said this place is the end of the earth and he's getting you out of here as soon as he bloody can.'

'Is that what he said?' Sophie grimaced in annoyance. It sounded exactly like Kevin. She picked Mandy up, chocolate mixture and all, and hugged her hard. 'Well, he's not taking me away for a while yet, sweetheart. Not until your Mary comes back. I'm going away for an hour or two now—no more.' She nodded, firming her decision. 'Moira, could you ring Reith and tell him what's happening? If there's anything seriously

medically wrong with Christabelle I'll need him. I'm
not licensed to practise in this country, and I sure as
heck don't have any equipment.'

'I'll tell him,' Moira agreed. 'Do you want him
to come?'

'No.' Sophie shook her head. 'The girl really does
sound over the edge and I'll find out what's wrong
first. If it's what I suspect, then I might not need
him at all.'

'What do you suspect?' Moira asked curiously.

'The most likely scenario is that she's been drinking
or has taken some drug she shouldn't. Another,
though, is that she's been raped,' Sophie said. 'They're
the three most common reasons for girls to react like
this and not let a parent near them. But it's just guesswork for now.'

Her guesswork was wrong.

It took ten long minutes before Sophie finally persuaded the terrified Christabelle to open the bedroom
door. She refused to open it a crack for her mother,
but finally, her mother firmly sent downstairs, she
opened the door an inch and a swollen, blotched face
peered out.

'I think I'm dying,' she whispered. 'Look at me.'

Sophie saw. The anxiety faded from her mind and
it was all she could do not to chuckle. Instead, she put
her hand through the crack and caught Christabelle's
hand, establishing a link.

'Can I come in?'

Christabelle looked at her for a long moment.
'You. . .you really are a doctor?'

'I really am a doctor.'

'Oh. . .' The girl turned and fled to the sanctuary
of her crumpled bedclothes. She hid her face in the
pillows and burst into noisy sobs. Sophie walked in,
shut the door firmly against Christabelle's mother and
sat down beside the bed. Then she waited.

It took five minutes for the hysterics to subside, and

they only did then because there was absolutely nothing feeding them. It was hard to keep up hysterical sobbing when no one was patting you on the shoulder, making sympathetic noises or responding in the slightest. Instead Sophie calmly waited for the paroxysms to subside.

Finally Christabelle turned her face up to Sophie, glanced wildly at her and buried her face in the pillows again.

'I wouldn't worry,' Sophie said evenly. 'I have seen chickenpox before.'

There was a deathly silence. The world appeared to hold its breath.

'Chickenpox. . . No! I don't believe you.' It was a faint thread of a whisper.

'Christabelle, I can see your neck and behind your ears from here. There are pustules which look for all the world like chickenpox, and there's a rash on your arms and legs that could be bigger by tomorrow.'

'Chickenpox. . .' The word echoed round and round the room while the girl took in the diagnosis and considered.

'I can't have chickenpox. I can't.' Christabelle's voice trembled. 'I thought I was dying of acne. If anyone sees me like this I'll die. I always have pimples and the girls tease me and these. . .' Her voice choked in revulsion.

'Are you feeling sick, too?' Sophie asked sympathetically.

'Yes! I feel awful!'

Sophie put her hand on the girl's forehead. She was running a fever. 'Dr Kenrick can give you something for the fever,' she told her. 'I don't know what's available in Australia or I'd tell you myself. He'll also be able to tell you what to put on your skin to stop the itch.'

Silence again. Then, 'You're sure it's chickenpox?'

'Almost a hundred per cent. It's a classic case, Christabelle.'

'And. . .and you think I should see Dr Kenrick?'

'I think it's only sensible. And I think we should tell your mum, too. She's very worried. She'll be very relieved it's something. . .' she had been about to say 'something simple' but caught herself in time; she just knew it was the wrong thing to say '. . .something we can treat,' she finished lamely.

Another silence.

'How long does it last?' Christabelle asked finally.

'Ten days to two weeks.'

The girl flung herself onto her back and stared out at Sophie from desperate eyes. 'I can't. . .I can't be like this for two weeks. . . And chickenpox! It's a kids' disease. How can I tell my friends I have chickenpox? I'll be a laughing stock.'

Sophie smiled, not without sympathy. 'How about telling them you have varicella? That's its true name. And I wouldn't worry about their laughing at you. Chickenpox—varicella—is incredibly contagious. Chances are that you'll be laughing at them in a week or two.'

'Really?'

'Really.'

'Varicella.' The girl looked up at Sophie in hope. 'Are there. . .are there complications?'

'Not often.'

'I'll read about it in Mum's medical dictionary.' The girl bounced off the bed and opened the door. 'Mum!'

She had inherited her mother's voice. The yell threatened to burst Sophie's eardrums.

Ten minutes later she was free to leave. Christabelle and her mother were happily buried in the *Family Medical Helper*, their tongues practising all the complications known to man—varicella haemorrhagica, varicella gangrenosa, ulceration, toxaemia, pneumonia, encephalitis. . .

'There's no way a healthy girl like you will suffer rare complications like those,' Sophie protested, only to be howled down.

'You can't be too careful,' Elvira pronounced solemnly. 'It's best to be prepared for the worst.'

Christabelle nodded in full agreement and Sophie suppressed a smile. Now the fears were behind them it was clear that Christabelle and her mother were about to dredge up every possible drop of drama from the situation.

She walked out into the sunshine and blinked. Reith Kenrick was sitting on the front stone fence, waiting for her.

'Nosing in on my patch, Dr Lynton?' he said quizzically, stretching his long legs into a standing position and intercepting her pathway to her car. 'And pinching my very favourite patients?'

'I'll bet they're your favourite patients.' Despite what the sight of the man was doing to her heartbeat, Sophie couldn't suppress a smile. 'You needn't worry. There's lots of medicine in store for you over the next two weeks from our Christabelle.'

'For instance?'

'Oh, I'd guess you'll be treating haemorrhage, toxaemia, ulceration, pneumonia. . .maybe even encephalitis.'

'What the deuce is wrong with the child?' Reith was clearly startled.

'Chickenpox.'

There was a moment of blank silence. Then Reith gave a shout of laughter. Sophie watched him, the pain inside twisting and twisting again into a hard knot. She found it almost impossible to laugh as well.

'You're kidding,' he finally grinned as laughter faded. 'From what Moira told me, I was expecting gang rape at the very least.'

'That's not listed as a chickenpox complication.'

Sophie smiled with a herculean effort. 'Oh, and it's not chickenpox, by the way. Varicella or nothing.'

'I'll remember.' Reith looked toward the house. 'Am I needed?'

'Give them time to make a list of complications and symptoms,' Sophie advised.

'You won't consider staying on as their personal medical adviser for two weeks?'

'No.'

It was a flat statement and Reith heard the misery behind it. He looked down at her.

'Your fiancé not making you happy, Dr Lynton?'

'What do you think?'

'People find happiness in the strangest of places.'

'And some people never find it at all.' She made to brush past him, but Reith reached forward and took her arm. His hand gripped the soft flesh of her forearm and Sophie gave an involuntary shiver.

The hand was withdrawn.

'I had a telephone call from Mary Vickers,' Reith said slowly. He was staring down at his hand, as if the touch to her arm had affected him in a way he didn't understand.

'And?' Sophie was staring at her car, unblinking. How could someone hurt so much when not physically wounded?

'She'll be here tomorrow morning to take Mandy home.'

'Good.' Sophie's voice softened. 'Mandy needs her.'

'And you and your Kevin will be able to go.'

'As you say.'

There was a long silence. It was as if there was a vast magnetic force pulling them together but each was standing rigid. If one moved an inch. . .

'I hope you'll be happy,' Reith said at last.

'You've said that before.' Finally Sophie made herself move. She walked across to her car and finally allowed herself a look back. 'I hope so, too,' she said softly. 'I doubt it, but at least I'm going to try. That's more than some people do. It's more than you do, Reith Kenrick. At least I have the courage to try.'

CHAPTER TEN

'WHERE the hell have you been?'

The accusation hit Sophie almost before she was out of the car. Kevin was waiting on the veranda, his face a mask of suppressed fury.

'I've been practising medicine,' Sophie told him wearily. She didn't have the energy to even try to deflect his anger. 'A case of. . .a case of varicella.'

'Varicella?' Kevin looked stunned. 'What the hell is that? And why can't the local doctor. . . Kenrick or whatever his name is. . .look after it?'

'They wanted a female doctor and I was available.'

'You're on holiday.'

'Yes,' Sophie said mildly. 'And so are you, Kevin. But you don't seem to have stopped work either.'

'That's different,' he snapped. 'You know damned well we depend on my income.'

'*We* don't,' Sophie said flatly. 'You do.'

'Well, what if we start a family? Look, Sophia, I've put work off for two weeks already—'

Kevin stopped dead, a trace of unease appearing behind the bluster. The suspicions Sophie had tried to ignore rammed home as solid fact.

'You put your work off for two weeks while you had holidays in Belgium,' Sophie said gently. 'In the time that was supposed to be our honeymoon.' She sighed, depression settling over her at the knowledge of what their relationship had become. 'Kevin, this is a farce.' She tugged the expensive diamond from the third finger of her left hand. 'And I think it's time we put an end to it.'

Kevin's jaw dropped a foot. The bluster sagged out of him.

'But Sophia. . .' He shook his head, searching for a response. 'I need you.'

Not 'I love you', but 'I need you'.

He did. Kevin was a mover and shaker and Sophie had been his security for a long time now—a place to prop up his ego and ready him for the next foray out into the exciting world. A world that included other women.

And Kevin had been security for Sophie.

'I needed you when I was seventeen,' Sophie said gently. 'Kevin, you were the family I never had, and I'm grateful. But I'm a big girl now and I have different needs. I need. . .I need to be treated as a person—to be loved as an equal. No matter what I do in life, with you I'll always be the little woman, waiting at home with slippers at the ready.' She bent forward and kissed him lightly on the lips. 'I've been your friend, Kevin. I'd like. . . I'd like to stay that way. But I don't want to be your wife. I don't want to be your woman.'

Kevin's face had been incredulous—stunned. As Sophie watched, it now ranged through the full gamut of emotions.

Anger won. It always would.

'You trollop,' Kevin gritted between his teeth. 'You lying little tart. It's Kenrick, isn't it?'

'Kevin, don't—'

'You're sleeping with him. You let me come all the way to Australia—'

'After you went all the way to Belgium to be with. . .with who, Kevin?'

'Is that what this is all about?' Kevin's face cleared. 'I don't know who the heck told you about her, but there's nothing in it. Sophia, I came here, didn't I? For heaven's sake, girl, I never offered to marry Jane. It's you I want.'

She hadn't wanted his infidelity thrown at her quite so baldly. Sophie took a step back and her hands rose to her face, as if in defence.

'Kevin, I don't want to hear about. . .about Jane.
And I haven't slept with Reith Kenrick,' she whispered. 'But it doesn't matter whether I have done or
not, because what's between us—you and me—is over.
I tried too late to stop you coming to Australia, but
when you did—well, I wondered whether there was
anything we could make a go of. There isn't. So. . .
so it's time you left. I'm sure you'll think of some way
to make the trip tax-deductible—or maybe. . .' by the
looks of his face, she guessed she had it right. 'Or
maybe you already have.'

She handed Kevin the ring, walked back to her car
and drove out of the guest-house grounds as fast as
she could.

She didn't look back.

It was late afternoon before Sophie finally ventured
home. She stopped at the gate, checking for Kevin's
Mercedes, and it wasn't until she'd assured herself it
was well and truly gone that she turned into the drive.

Mandy catapulted from the house as a relieved little
whirlwind.

'Sophie, you said you'd only be an hour or two,' the
child accused. 'And you've been hours and hours and
Mrs Sanderson said you came back while I was having
a nap but I didn't see you and she said you and Mr
Carson had a. . .a difference of opinion. . .and you
drove off again—and Mrs Sanderson said she bets she
knows why—and Mr Carson's gone and Mrs
Sanderson says he won't be missed, and I don't miss
him at all but he's your friend, isn't he, Sophie?'

Sophie climbed out of the car and took Mandy's
small hands in hers. She looked at where the Mercedes
had been. There was no regret. She should have done
this years ago. She should have had the courage.

And Reith Kenrick's given it to me, she told herself
softly. Even if. . .even if he can't return my love,
maybe he's done me a massive favour.

So she should remember Reith with gratitude?

She could remember Reith Kenrick with nothing but aching, desolate loss for what might have been.

'You look really sad,' Mandy said solemnly, tugging her inside the house. 'Don't be sad, Sophie. Mrs Sanderson and me didn't like Mr Carson very much anyway. And we've made the most enormous chocolate cake and put on heaps and heaps of icing and Mrs Sanderson wouldn't let me have even the littlest, littlest bit until you came home—so that has to cheer you up, doesn't it?'

'It sure should,' Sophie agreed, reaching down to give Mandy a hard hug. 'It sure should.'

Mary Vickers arrived on Sunday morning to relieve Sophie of her last responsibility. There was no mistaking her suitability as a mother for the little girl. Mary drove into the guest-house driveway, and Mandy flew out of the door and into her arms like an arrow straight to her heart.

From the veranda Sophie watched them, woman and child, clinging together with the fierceness of absolute possession. Heaven help the social worker who tries to part these two now, she thought and knew that it would never happen.

Her thoughts were backed by Mary two minutes later.

'I didn't like leaving Ted,' Mary Vickers confessed, 'but he insisted. Mandy's been our little girl from the time she moved next door. Her dad's been so ill—if it hadn't been for us the welfare people would have whisked her away months ago. Though it might have been better if they had.'

'You can't blame yourselves for what happened,' Sophie said gently. 'You weren't to know.'

'No.' Mary shook her head. 'He was such a nice boy, Mandy's dad. When he was well he tried so hard. It was only when the illness took over that he couldn't cope and Mandy needed us. And this way. . .well, Mandy had her dad for four years and that's more than a lot of kids have.'

Sophie nodded. This would be OK. Mandy would grow up being reminded of her father with love and the terrors of that one awful night would drift into unimportance.

'We're just so grateful to Dr Kenrick—and to you, too, of course,' Mary said. 'You both saved Ted's life. And then Dr Kenrick. . .to go to all that trouble. . .'

'Trouble?'

'He's spent hours and hours over the past few days arguing with Social Welfare—giving us time. He told them Mandy was ill but safe and not to be disturbed until tomorrow—and tomorrow I'll have her tucked up in her own little bedroom at home. It's a shame Ted won't be with me but Dr Kenrick has dispositions from all sorts of respectable people telling Social Welfare what good parents we'd make, how much time we've spent with Mandy already and how much we love her. He's organized certificates from the *in vitro* fertilization people saying we've been trying to have a baby for ages, and located the forms from when we applied for adoption years ago. The welfare services judged us suitable then—but there wasn't a baby available and now we've passed the right age. I don't know where Dr Kenrick's dug all these forms from. He seems to have people all over the state working for us. I even had a doctor contact me who Dr Kenrick persuaded to go into the IV clinic yesterday—*Saturday*—to collect files.' Her eyes filled with tears. 'Doc Kenrick. . .well, he's the most wonderful doctor, the most wonderful person I know, and, thanks to him, Ted and I will have our Mandy.'

They went off together soon after, Mandy sitting as close to her Mary as the seat belt would permit, and Sophie blinked back tears as she watched them go.

Happy ever after for one little girl and two

loving parents—because of Reith Kenrick.

She wanted a happy ever after, too.

'And now what about you, Sophie, girl?' Moira asked as they watched the receding car. 'You're shot of that fiancé for good, I hope?'

'I guess I am,' Sophie said dully and Moira stared.

'You're never pining for him, are you, girl?'

'N-no.'

'I should think not. That man was a user if ever I saw one, and a woman is better off with no man than one who treats her as a doormat.'

'I know. I should. . .I should have seen it years ago.'

'But you didn't want to be alone. And now you're alone again and it's scaring you,' Moira guessed. She peered closer at Sophie's closed face. 'But that's not all that's making you miserable, is it, Sophie, dear?' Her eyes narrowed. 'It wouldn't be. . .' She took a deep breath as though daring herself to continue. 'It wouldn't be our Dr Kenrick, would it, Sophie?'

'No.'

The calm grey eyes didn't lose their intentness. 'Liar,' Moira said evenly and smiled. Her eyes were bright with the trace of tears from bidding Mandy goodbye and now they glistened in sympathy. 'Oh, Sophie. . .'

Sophie shook her head. 'Moira, I'm twenty-eight years old. You sound as if I'm ten. I'm old enough to know better than to fall head over heels for a man who needs a woman like he needs a new truck!'

She heard what she'd said. Sophie caught her breath and gasped and Moira broke into a delighted chuckle.

'That man needs a truck nearly as much as he needs a woman,' she pronounced. 'And that's desperately.'

'He won't buy one.'

'He will eventually. And he'll realise there are women he can trust. A woman. . .'

'I bet he can patch up that old truck with string and glue for years yet,' Sophie said darkly.

'Someone could sabotage it,' Moira suggested. 'Maybe the same thing can be done for his need of a woman. Maybe there's sabotage already afoot—making our Dr Kenrick realise just how bleak his life is without you.'

'I. . .I don't know what you mean.'

'I mean, you're not planning on leaving here right this minute, are you, dear?' Moira asked blandly.

'I should.'

'But you won't.' Moira smiled with affection. 'And I'll help any way I can. Sophie, for your information, I've stopped charging you for accommodation. I charged your horrid Kevin like a wounded bull, and he's more than covered expenses for both of you. So from now on you're here as my guest. Just for a day or two,' she begged. 'Just till you get the stitches out of your arm. I don't like the idea of you driving all the way to Melbourne with stitches in your arm.'

'I should go. . .'

'But you'll stay?'

'Moira, there is no chance of anything happening between me and Reith Kenrick. No chance in a million years.'

'If you go now there won't be,' Moira said darkly. 'A coward would walk away. But a girl who's fighting for a future that's important to her. . .'

'He won't even see me.'

'He won't see you if you're in England.' Moira spread her hands. 'Two days, Sophie. The rest will do you good, without your dratted Kevin. Two days to swim and sleep and walk and think about your future. It makes sense to me. How about it?'

She didn't leave. Of course she didn't leave. To get in the car and head back to the airport would be like ripping herself apart, and mutilation wasn't something Sophie was good at. She swam and walked and let her tired mind rest, and to her amazement on Sunday night she slept like a baby. If she couldn't have Reith, it seemed that the decision to shed herself of Kevin was a good one.

She slept late on Monday morning, swam and walked again, but by mid-afternoon she was starting to get restless. She wasn't good at holidays. She didn't know what the heck to do with them.

She sat on Reith's swing with a book, trying hard to concentrate on the murder mystery in front of her, but the words wouldn't focus. She read the same page three times before Moira emerged from the house and she looked up in relief.

'Are you busy?' Moira called.

'Frantically.' Sophie threw the book aside in disgust. 'Right in the middle of an action-packed afternoon. What can I do for you?'

'Well. . .' Moira took a deep breath as though searching for courage. 'It's what you might do for Dr Kenrick.'

'What I might do?' Sophie stood up. 'Exactly. . . exactly what did you have in mind, Moira Sanderson?'

'Now, I'm not plotting.' Moira wiped her hands on her tea-towel as she walked across the lawn to the swing. 'It's just. . .there's some drama going on up at the school and I thought. . .I thought you might like to help.'

'Drama?'

'My friend Muriel lives next door to the school,' Moira explained. 'She rang just then. It seems. . .it seems they have an epidemic on their hands. A girl fainted and had to be taken out of class and then another and there are about fifteen girls affected at the moment with vomiting and fainting and more by the minute, and Reith's on his way, but Muriel just rang to say he might need you if you were still here.'

Her voice rose in an absurd, birdlike expression of hope. She stood looking so much like a nonchalant sparrow that Sophie burst into laughter.

'Moira Sanderson, you are as transparent as glass.'

'I'm not making this up,' Moira said, wounded.

'You swear?'

'Scout's honour.' She held up three floury fingers. 'Why don't you just go down there and see?'

'Why don't I just ring the headmaster and see if they need me?'

Moira brightened. 'Oh, yes. The headmaster's Jenny's husband—David Lee. A nice, sensible man, but it sounds as if he'll really need you.'

He did. The headmaster's response was sharp and to the point.

'I don't know what the hell is going on,' he told Sophie, clearly desperate to finish fast on the phone and get back to his crisis. 'But they're certainly ill and I don't think one doctor can cope. Dr Kenrick's here and we've called for ambulances from Lamberton but—'

'I'll be right there,' Sophie told him. The phone crashed down before she finished speaking.

Sophie didn't stop to change, deciding that jeans and blouse would do in a crisis. She drove herself. Moira had scones in the oven, and clearly didn't regard vomiting teenagers worth burnt scones.

'It'll be them dratted hot dogs they sell in the school canteen that's done it,' she pronounced darkly. 'You see if I'm right. You just have to look at the colour of them to know they're disgusting. The last one someone tried to give me was bright pink. Pink food! The blasted sausage was so plastic you could tie a knot in it without it breaking. You can't tell me kids can eat those things without muddling their insides.'

Food poisoning. It could be, Sophie thought as she drove down into the little town. A batch of bad meat. . .

There was a teacher in the front office, clearly sent to wait for her. She took Sophie's arm with relief and led her through to the backyard.

'We've put them outside,' the teacher told her. 'In the shade of the trees. We thought if it's infectious they're better in the open. We've asked the parents of non-affected children to take them home.'

Sensible precautions—as long as the children sent home didn't develop symptoms. Sophie had a nightmare flash of children all through the mountains becoming ill.

If it was food poisoning then the problems depended on what sort it was. A staphylococcal poisoning produced symptoms almost immediately and they'd quickly know the extent of the problem—but if the bacterium causing problems was salmonella then symptoms could occur between twelve to thirty-six hours after eating.

'Is Dr Kenrick here?'

'Yes. He got here fast.'

He would. This could be a real disaster. 'Does he think it's food poisoning?'

'I don't know.' The young teacher seemed really distressed. She seized Sophie's arm tighter before they went through the outside door. 'Dr Lynton. . .'

'What's wrong?' Sophie asked gently, seeing the fear.

'N. . .nothing. Well. . .well, I think I'm about seven weeks pregnant. I haven't had a pregnancy test yet but I'm pretty sure and. . .and we do want this baby. I've had two miscarriages already. If I catch whatever the girls have. . .'

Sophie stopped dead. She turned to the woman and noted her pale, fearful face. 'Do you have any symptoms?'

'N. . .no. I vomited this morning—but then. . . I've vomited every morning this week.'

Sophie smiled. 'They reckon morning sickness is a sign of a robust baby,' she said firmly. She caught the girl's hands. 'Still, I agree, it's no use taking chances. I think you should go home now and stay home until we figure out just what's going on here. OK?'

'OK.'

The girl went. Sophie watched her retreat, took a deep breath and opened the door outside.

Good grief.

There were bodies everywhere. Girls. . .they were all teenage girls by the look of it, some hysterical, some moaning and clutching their stomachs and one girl hunched into a foetal position screaming that she was going to die. A couple of teachers moved help-lessly among them—and staring out over the whole disaster, his brow as black as thunder, was Reith Kenrick.

Sophie walked quietly up to him and touched his arm. 'What needs to be done?'

Reith turned to her, incredulity written in every line of his face. 'You!'

The word made Sophie cringe. There was no delight here that she wasn't back in England as he'd thought.

'It looks as if you need help,' she managed.

'You might say that.' Reith's mouth was set in a tight, hard line.

'Do you know what's happening?'

'I think I do.' He turned to the girls. 'Let's see if you can discover it, too, Dr Lynton?'

Sophie's green eyes flashed anger. What stupid game was this? 'Do you mind telling me what's going on?'

He smiled then, his smile sardonic and angry. 'You try answering a few questions, Dr Lynton. For instance, what do we appear to have here?'

Sophie frowned, gazing over the sprawled bodies. 'Fifteen or so girls—'

'Funny, that,' Reith snapped. 'No boys. Ages?'

Once more Sophie stared. The girls were all in their young teens—thirteen to fifteen, at a guess. 'Teenagers.'

'That's right. Teenagers. We have a comprehensive school of both sexes from four to seventeen, yet the only ones ill are thirteen- and fourteen-year-old girls. There's been no party or gathering of the girls where they might have eaten the same food. Their symptoms—apart from the odd hysteria-induced vomit—seem to be fainting, clutching of stomachs, threatening to die and wanting their mothers. Suggest anything to you, Dr Lynton?'

'Hysteria,' Sophie said slowly. She'd seen it before. One teenage girl became genuinely ill and the rest of the group went out in sympathy—not deliberately to gain attention, but because they genuinely believed they were ill.

'Do you know what's triggering this?' she asked cautiously.

'You.'

Sophie gaped. 'I beg your pardon?'

'You gave Christabelle Pilkington varicella. Not nice, common or garden chickenpox, but awful, life-threatening, scars-for-life varicella. The complications are horrible, I hear. Encephalitis, haemorrhage, pneumonia, sterility—'

'Where did she get sterility?' Sophie gasped, finally realising what Reith was talking about. 'It's not a known complication—'

'So you did tell her the complications?'

'She looked them up in the medical encyclopaedia. I didn't give them to her.' Sophie's voice was practically a wail.

'But you did tell her she had varicella instead of chickenpox?'

'It made her feel better.'

'Well, I gather,' Reith said dangerously, 'that our Christabelle has spent the entire weekend telephoning her friends, telling them what a ghastly, potentially fatal and highly contagious disease she'd just gone down with. It took a few hours of the girls' being together and comparing symptoms before some of them started feeling very strange indeed. Then someone heard someone vomiting in the women's toilets and there you are. They collapsed like ninepins.'

'Oh.' Sophie stared, daunted, out over the moaning throng. 'Oh. . .'

Her lips twitched. She tried really hard. . .

It was impossible. Before she could stop herself, Sophie burst into a peal of delighted laughter. Catastrophe turned to farce in ten split-seconds.

The teachers were staring up at her as if she had gone mad.

'Are you quite done?'

Reith's voice was like a douche of cold water. Only a faint crease at the corners of his eyes told her that he, too, saw the ridiculous side of the situation. 'It's hardly the time for levity, Dr Lynton.'

Sophie bit her lip and managed to assume an expression of suitable solemnity. 'No, Dr Kenrick. What. . .what should we do now?'

He flashed her a suspicious look, hearing the laughter threading through her voice. 'I should leave you with the whole mess.'

'I'll get onto the first plane back to England,' she threatened and her lips twitched compulsively.

'Laugh once more, and I'll throw cold water on you.'

'We could do that to the lot of them.'

Reith shook his head glumly. 'Wouldn't work. They all genuinely think they're ill. The symptoms are so genuine that it took me six examinations before I was sure I was right.'

'So. . .'

He sighed. 'So we see each of them individually. Alone. Without any of them feeding hysteria off the others. We tell them exactly what's wrong with Christabelle; bother the girl's nicer feelings—it's going to be chickenpox. We suggest that what they're experiencing might be the first symptom of chickenpox so that they come out of this with some pride intact, and then we send them home with individual parents. And we tell the individual parents what's going on.'

'It'll take hours,' Sophie said, horrified.

'Well, maybe you should have caught your plane back to England yesterday,' Reith said darkly. 'Because if you leave now, before this mess is sorted out, I'll drag you back by the hair of your head. Caveman stuff, Dr Lynton. Now, shall we put these teachers out of their misery and get on with it?'

'I suppose so,' Sophie said doubtfully.

'There's no "suppose". Move, Dr Lynton.'

It was three long hours before the last girl departed with her parents. The final girl had clung persistently to her symptoms, growing more and more agitated at every attempt to calm her. Finally Reith had administered a sedative.

'Take her home and let her sleep it off,' he told the girl's over-anxious parents. 'Telephone me in the morning if she's not clear of symptoms.'

Finally they were left in the bare staff-room, looking at the debris of blankets and muddle left from the chaos.

'That's that,' Reith said wearily. 'Let me know when you're intending to diagnose varicella in the near future, Dr Lynton. I'll go on holidays.'

Sophie smiled and shook her head. 'I won't.' Even if she did, it wouldn't worry Reith. She'd be back in England.

He looked across at her. 'So. . .you and Kevin are still enjoying your holiday, then?' It was a casual question, carefully phrased.

'Kevin's gone home.'

There was a long silence.

'More business?' Reith said finally. 'You're not having much luck with your honeymoon, Dr Lynton.'

'No.' Sophie stood up. 'I have to go.' She walked toward the door but stopped as the harassed-looking headmaster walked through the door.

'All finished?'

'Yes,' Reith told him. He glanced at his watch. 'I'm overdue for clinic. We'll leave you to it.'

'Thank you both,' the headmaster said gratefully. He hesitated. 'There is one thing, though.'

'Yes?'

'Our young maths teacher. . . Lisa Carvis. Dr Lynton sent her home and I wondered why. Was she ill? Surely Lisa wouldn't be influenced by the general hysteria?'

'Oh. . .' Sophie bit her lip. She'd forgotten the frightened young woman.

'Why on earth did you send her home?' Reith demanded, and Sophie thought fast. It wasn't her place to tell these two men that the young teacher was pregnant.

'Lisa really did have an upset stomach, but her symptoms were different from the girls'—and totally genuine,' she said finally. 'She was ill this morning— in fact, her vomiting might have triggered the rest off. With the fuss happening here she was safer at home.'

'But. . .' The headmaster was clearly puzzled.

'I'll go and see her at home now if you'll give me her address,' Sophie said quickly, trying to deflect the queries she saw behind the headmaster's frown.

Reith nodded thoughtfully at her. 'You do that, Dr Lynton. It can be your final atonement for creating this mess.' He smiled at her then and the smile softened the severity of his words. It took Sophie's heart away all over again. 'And then come back and report to my clinic.'

'I'll telephone.'

'The clinic's on your way home from Lisa's,' Reith said firmly. 'I want to talk to you in person before you go home.'

Sophie took a deep breath. 'Yes, sir,' she said faintly and raised two fingers in mock salute. 'Any more orders?'

'That'll be all for now, Dr Lynton,' Reith grinned. 'Dismissed.'

CHAPTER ELEVEN

IT WAS a fast process to reassure Lisa.

The girl listened carefully to Sophie's explanation and, like Sophie, burst into relieved and delighted laughter.

'Oh, and I've already had the chickenpox. I could have stayed and helped. What on earth will the rest of the teachers think of me, turning tail and running?'

'They'll understand when they know you're pregnant.'

'Mmm.' Lisa patted her very flat stomach with complacency. 'Well, I won't tell them about junior for a while yet—just in case—but I have a good feeling about this pregnancy.'

'You know something?' Sophie smiled. 'So do I.'

'You don't fancy staying around for the next few months, I suppose?' Lisa asked shyly. 'I wouldn't mind a woman doctor.'

Sophie's smile faded. 'I wish I could,' she said softly. 'I just wish I could.'

Reith was still seeing patients when Sophie arrived at his clinic. He motioned her to a chair and a pile of magazines.

'I'm in a hurry,' Sophie said abruptly. 'I'd rather just tell you about Lisa and go.'

'I'd like to talk to you, though, Dr Lynton.' Reith had picked up his next patient's card and was ushering an elderly man into his surgery. 'I telephoned Moira and told her you'd be late—so there's no hurry at all.'

'But—'

'Could you come right in, Mr Hardcastle?'

He assisted Mr Hardcastle through the door and

157

closed it, leaving Sophie fairly gnashing her teeth after him.

She could leave a nasty note and walk out. . .

The patients still waiting smiled at her with friendly interest. Sophie's presence hadn't gone unnoticed in the district, it seemed, and she was very welcome.

It would be childish to scrawl angry words and stalk out.

Did she really want to?

Sabotage. . .

Moira's word flew into her head. Moira had suggested she should sabotage Reith's lonely future by refusing to go. By clinging and hoping. . .

This wasn't sabotage. This was Reith Kenrick wanting to see her. Sophie gave a virtuous sniff, smiled round at the curious faces and picked up the *Woman's Mirror*.

'I didn't think you'd wait.'

The last patient had finally gone. Reith walked out, closed his surgery door behind him and lifted the magazine from Sophie's fingers.

'Do you mind?' Sophie demanded indignantly. 'Lorissa's about to confess to Jed she's not really his sister, and Dave, who Jed thinks is Lorissa's lover, is Lorissa's best friend's husband and what's the bet Jed and Lorissa fall straight into each others' arms and live happily ever after?'

Reith grinned. He held the magazine open to where she'd been reading and, with one deft pull, ripped out the page. Folding it with care, he tucked it down the unbuttoned neckline of her blouse.

'There you are, Dr Lynton. Never let it be said that I came between star-crossed lovers.'

'Oh, great,' Sophie said. Her voice sounded slightly breathless. The folded paper was sliding down against her bare skin and it was as though Reith was touching her. 'Now the rest of your patients will get to the last page and find the happy ending gone.'

'That's life,' Reith said sagely. 'It's time you had those stitches out, Dr Lynton.'

'Is that why you wanted me to wait? I can very well take them out myself.'

'I like to check my own handiwork. Sit down.'

Sophie glared.

'Sophie. . .' He shook his head as he would at an exasperating child. 'Do you want to sit or do you want to be sat?'

'Neither.'

'I'll bribe you with jelly beans if you like.' He smiled and Sophie's heart twisted within. 'There's really nothing to fear,' he said kindly.

'I'm not scared.'

'Then sit down.'

She sat. There seemed little else she could do.

Reith bent over the stitches, his small surgical scissors working with care. 'Very nice,' he said, admiring the neat line of scarring he revealed as the stitches fell away. 'Even if I do say so myself.'

'If you don't praise yourself, who will?' Sophie asked with careful sarcasm, and Reith grinned.

'Very true.' He snipped the last stitch. 'Great. Now, Dr Lynton, suppose you answer a few of my questions?'

'L-like what?'

'Like, why did you send Lisa home from school?'

'I was worried she'd catch what the girls had.'

'Why?'

Sophie shrugged. 'I can't tell you that, Dr Kenrick.'

Reith nodded. 'Very professional. How many weeks pregnant is she—and why on earth hasn't she seen me yet?'

Sophie raised her eyebrows. 'That's pure supposition, Dr Kenrick, and you know you're treading on professional ethics by asking.' She relented a little. 'But I wouldn't be surprised if you saw her tomorrow.'

'Excellent.' He smiled down at her. 'I have to tell

you that was a fine spot of counselling back at the school, Dr Lynton. If you hadn't caused the whole drama, I'd say you'd done very well indeed.'

'How kind,' Sophie snapped. 'Can I go now. . .sir?'

'I have another question.'

'Well, ask it fast.'

'Where's Kevin?'

Sophie winced.

That *he* should ask. . . Reith, who had pulled her life apart.

'I have no idea,' she said bleakly. She stood abruptly. 'Thank you for removing the stitches. I'll go now.'

Reith reached forward and took her hand in his. He lifted her ring finger.

'Not engaged any more, Sophie?'

'What do you think?'

'I think. . .' he showed no sign of releasing her fingers, and his eyes held her even closer '. . .I think we might go out for dinner again, Dr Lynton. On unengaged terms.'

'Unengaged?'

'Without Kevin in the background,' he said simply. 'For both of us.'

Sophie took a deep breath. The world stood still. Please. . .

'I'd like that,' she said simply. 'Very much.'

Reith didn't take her to a restaurant. He made a fast telephone call, led Sophie out to the truck and drove north, high into the mountains. Five minutes from town, he stopped outside a cottage, left Sophie in the car while he went inside and re-emerged carrying a laden picnic basket.

'From one of my patients,' he explained, seeing Sophie's look of astonishment. 'Gilda's Gourmet Goodies. Bush picnics are Gilda's specialty.'

'Is that what we're having? A picnic?'

'We sure are. In my very favourite place.'

It was the place where *Bush Bride* had been painted.

Sophie climbed out of the truck and gazed around in awe. Such a place! She hadn't dreamed such a place existed. The painting had been magnificent in its beauty, but no painting could approach this. The tiny lake reflected the mountains around as though the world were upside-down. The sun was setting over the distant peaks, and crimson fire was everywhere.

'I thought we'd make it in time,' Reith said in quiet satisfaction. 'Sunset is the best.'

Sophie didn't answer. She was absorbing the beauty into her heart. How could she leave this place? How could she? The splendour went on and on—endless in its loveliness.

Endless. . .

'Sophie.' Reith swung her round to face him. 'Don't cry, Sophie,' he said gently. He put a finger up and wiped a tear from her cheek.

'I'm not c-crying. I never cry. It's just. . .it's just that it's so beautiful.'

'It is, isn't it?' Reith agreed, and he wasn't looking at the scenery.

'D-don't.' She pushed his hand away, unable to bear it. This beauty and Reith—here, now. . . How could she not reveal what was in heart?

'P-please. . .are we here to eat?'

He stood looking down at her, his face grave. Finally he nodded.

'OK, Sophie,' he said gently. 'We're here to eat.'

The picnic was perfect—homemade quiche still warm from the oven, crispy rolls, avocado and lemon and some sort of lettuce that was frilled with purple and tasted of basil and oregano and indefinable herbs that Sophie couldn't identify and was too absorbed to try.

Despite the delectable food, Sophie ate little, and ended up feeding most of her salad to the wallabies that swarmed around them as soon as the picnic was produced.

'Since this has become a national park the kangaroos and wallabies have emerged from the bush in their hundreds,' Reith told her. 'It's as if they know guns have now been banned.'

Sophie smiled. She was lying full-length on her stomach, hand-feeding a tiny joey whose nose just emerged from his mother's pouch. The mother wallaby was holding a lettuce leaf between two dainty paws, nibbling in contentment and watching her baby being fed with maternal indulgence.

'I wish Kevin could have seen this,' Sophie said impulsively and then wished she hadn't.

Reith was packing up the last of the picnic. The sun was sliding down behind the mountains, only a sliver of tangerine and gold on the horizon now marking its path. The night was descending with the softness of velvet.

'You'll miss him?'

Sophie shook her head. 'No. No, I won't.'

'Then why were you going to marry him?'

It was a fair question. Sophie broke her last remaining lettuce leaf into shreds, eking out her baby's feed to last as long as possible.

'I guess. . .I guess Kevin was my security,' she said at last. 'Security seemed important.'

'So I was right?' Reith said drily. 'You moved from the security of your parents to the security of Kevin.'

'Not quite.'

There was a silence. Reith corked the wine bottle and replaced it in the basket. Sophie finished her feeding and then turned over on the picnic rug to lie on her back. She put her hands behind her head and looked up to the heavens. The evening star was just twinkling into existence.

'You're not the only one who had a bad childhood,' Sophie said at last. 'My mum. . .well, the only use I was to my mum was as leverage for money from my father. I was in her way. My father didn't want to

know me and threw money at me to ease his conscience. Kevin came along when I was seventeen. He
gave me an anchor that I'd never had, and I desperately
needed it.'

'And now you've sent your anchor back to England.'

'That's right.'

'So where does that leave you, my Sophie?'

My Sophie. . . The words drifted on the night and
Sophie closed her eyes. If only she was.

'I don't know,' she whispered. 'I don't. . .' The pain
in her words was there for him to hear. She couldn't
hide it. The gentle night enfolded her, but the pain
was still there.

'Sophie. . .'

He moved then, leaning forward so that his arms
were on either side of her, and he was looking down
into her face. She opened her eyes and he was between
her eyes and the stars.

'Reith,' she whispered. 'Reith. . .'

For one long moment he held out against her appeal.
Her face was white in the twilight and her eyes were
drowning pools of pain. He put a finger on her hair
and twisted a curl around and around.

The magnet was there, pulling so hard. . .pulling. . .

He'd be less than human if he resisted that pull.

With a groan Reith sank to gather her close, letting
the magnet do its will.

The magnet's force was supreme. Sophie was powerless to move as Reith's head lowered over hers and
his lips gently claimed hers. She didn't want to move.
Her hands closed over his dark hair, deepening the
kiss, tasting and wanting this man so much that her
whole body cried with desire.

She had felt this way since she'd first met him. Her
body was his body, and his body hers.

One. Two halves of a whole. How could she feel
like this and Reith not feel the same?

His tongue was moving into her mouth and she welcomed the taste of him with joy. His hands were searching for the buttons of her blouse. She arched slightly, helping him, wanting him. . .

Then his fingers were on her breasts, touching the nipples, taunting them into peaked and throbbing points of fire. When his head moved and his lips fell downward to gently caress and kiss it was all she could do not to cry out with joy.

Joy and sadness. This was her place. This was her man and she was Reith's woman as surely now as if he had placed a wedding band on the third finger of her left hand. Reith was making no promises, she knew, and maybe. . .maybe what was happening here would have to last for the rest of her life.

So be it. If this was all she could have of Reith she would take it with gratitude and with love—and she would live with this night in her heart forever.

He drew back then, one hand still gently cupping her breast.

'Sophie. . .' He whispered her name and gently kissed her on the lips. 'God knows I shouldn't, Sophie, but I want you. . .I want you as I've wanted no woman before.'

'I love you, Reith,' she told him simply.

That stilled him. His body stayed motionless. 'Sophie, I can't—'

'You don't believe you can love?' She smiled tenderly up at him, loving him with every fibre of her body. 'I know. It doesn't stop me loving you, Reith Kenrick. Tomorrow. . .tomorrow I'll leave and be gone from your life forever, but for tonight. . .tonight I'm your bush bride, Reith. Yours. I promise you no strings, but tonight my love is yours, and I want you more than I've ever wanted anything in my life. And maybe. . .maybe my love is strong enough for both of us.'

'Dear God. . .' He groaned, his body rigid above her. 'I should take you home now. This is madness.'

'I wouldn't go, Reith Kenrick,' Sophie whispered, her fingers carefully unbuttoning the front of his shirt. 'You'd have to drive me with a whip and even then I'd cling and cry. So, you see. . .you'll just have to make love to me, my love. . .whether or not you want to.'

'Sophie—'

'You're wasting time with your protests,' she whispered. 'You know you want me. You know the force pulling us together is stronger than both of us.'

He smiled then, his lean face twisting into gentle, uncertain laughter. 'You shameless woman!'

'I am, aren't I?' She laughed up at him, marvelling at herself even as she spoke. Was this really Sophie Lynton—this woman offering her body without shame? This woman fighting for what was hers with every fibre of her soul? This woman working sabotage as though her life depended on it?

Her life did depend on it. If the fight was lost, what was left?

'And if I make you pregnant?'

There would be nothing but joy, Sophie thought, to carry Reith Kenrick's child.

'I'm protected,' she told him, and her voice held a trace of regret.

He pulled her into a sitting position, his fathomless eyes holding hers in the light of the rising moon. His face searched hers.

'You're sure of this, my Sophie?'

'It's the only thing I am sure of,' Sophie whispered. 'I'm only sure that I want this. For tonight. . .this is right. You must feel it, too.'

'I do feel it,' he said roughly. 'You drive me to the edge of madness, Sophie Lynton. A sane man would get into his truck and drive away fast—right now.'

'A sane man would never get in your truck,' she teased him and watched his eyes crease into laughter.

'Wanton. . .' His hands lifted her blouse from her shoulders.

'Yes,' she whispered in agreement.

'Shameless. . .' Somehow her jeans were disappearing and she felt them go with pleasure.

'That too.'

'Beautiful. . . Bewitching. . .' His eyes were devouring her, making love to her without so much as touching her, and her body was on fire.

'If you say so. Reith?'

'Mmm.'

'Shut up and love me.'

'If you say so, ma'am.'

He pulled her to him with a savage groan, and suddenly it was no longer Sophie who was doing the seducing. Reith was in control, taking his love with a fierceness of possession and joy that left Sophie breathless.

Her arms pulled him tighter, tighter as skin met against skin.

Her love. . . Her love and her life. . .

For this moment and for always.

The twilight faded into darkness, the moon rose to look serenely down on two bush lovers and the night enfolded them with the magic of love.

Sophie woke some time after midnight. Something was wrong. Something.

It wasn't where she was that was the problem. Sophie was enfolded in the curve of Reith's body, wrapped in a cocoon of soft blanket and Reith's arms. She could feel the warm curve of him, and his arms holding her with a possessiveness even in sleep.

The night was warm and still, and just out of arm's reach the wallabies were grazing on the lush grass.

It was the telephone. Here of all places. Its strident ring was sounding from the truck and Reith groaned and stirred.

No. . .

She didn't say it. Sophie's whole body screamed it, but duty had been instilled too deeply in her by her medical training to do what she would like to do— hurl the dratted telephone to the bottom of the lake.

Reith was this district's only doctor. He had to answer it.

He swore softly, his arms lingering for a fraction of a moment on the softness of Sophie's body, and then pulled away, reaching for his trousers in the dark.

'I wouldn't worry about dressing for the telephone.' Sophie smiled into the night. 'The wallabies don't seem to be shocked—and they've seen worse tonight.'

Reith chuckled but his mind was on the telephone. Swiftly he strode across to answer it.

Sophie lay as quiet as a mouse, saying a silent prayer that wasn't answered.

'What?'

'Chest pain,' Reith said regretfully. He returned and reached down to pull Sophie to her feet. 'Duty calls, my love.'

'I'll stay in bed and wait for you.' Sophie smiled but knew before she said it what his answer would be.

'If I'm delayed you'll still be here in the morning— and all you need is a troop of local scouts dib-dibbing through here at six a.m. to be in a real pickle.' He grinned and pulled her up close to him, his hands caressing the nakedness of her thighs. 'Let's get you dressed, Dr Lynton, and I'll take you home.'

Home. . .

Sophie just knew whose home it would be. Not Reith's.

She sat silently beside him in the awful truck, cold and increasingly fearful. Reith's face, in the dim light, was an intent and distant mask—as though he had put away something beautiful with regret, but with finality. Now on with the rest of his life.

She knew she was right when he stopped in Moira's

front yard. He pulled her into his arms and kissed her
with the fierceness and passion of a man going to war.
A man leaving his woman—maybe forever.

'Goodbye, Sophie,' he said roughly as he finally put
her away from him. He touched her face. 'You're the
most beautiful woman I've ever known. I wish to
God. . .' He shook his head. 'I wish to God it could
somehow work.'

'You won't risk trying to make it work?' Sophie's
voice was trembling. Despite the heat of the night, she
felt cold to the marrow.

'Sophie, it's going to be bad enough when you
leave now.'

'I don't have to leave.' She sounded about six,
Sophie thought. Bereft.

'Yeah. . .' Reith's tone changed. All of a sudden he
was the bushman again—the stranger Sophie had first
met. Cynicism dropped down like a shield. 'You don't
have to leave tomorrow. But you will have to leave
eventually. You're booked on a plane tomorrow, so
you might as well get on with it.'

'Let me stay.' Dear God, was that Sophie speaking—independent career woman? Pleading for her
future?

Pride and love. . . They were as opposite as black
and white and there was no mingling grey.

He laughed then, a harsh, cynical laugh that hurt.
'No.' He turned and caught her hands. 'Hell, Sophie,
I should never have let things go this far. I've been a
selfish bastard—but then, that's what I have to be
because when you finally go. . .if you stayed and got
any closer to me. . .' He sighed. 'I think I'd go mad.'

'I'm going mad, anyway,' Sophie whispered.

'Then the sooner you leave, the sooner the
pain stops.'

'Is that what you really think?'

'Yes.'

He was wrong. The sooner she left, the sooner the

pain started. It was here now, knifing through her with an agony worse than any chest pain.

He had a patient to go to. He had his life.

Without her. . .

Sophie clenched her fingers into her palms so hard that she broke the skin. Then, somehow, she made herself open her eyes, lean forward and kiss him very softly on the lips.

'You know where I am if you ever need me,' she whispered softly. 'England's only half a world away—'

Her voice broke on a sob. She couldn't bear it. Reith's hands came out to hold her but she was too fast for him.

Somehow she was out of the truck, the door slamming behind her, and she was stumbling up the veranda and into the sanctuary of her bedroom.

Reith was left staring after her, his face as bleak and hard as ever.

Moira greeted her at breakfast with quiet concern.

'You look dreadful, girl,' she said frankly. 'What happened?'

Sophie shrugged. She poured herself a coffee and took a sip. It tasted of mud—yet it was the beautiful percolated brew that Sophie had tasted at other times with delight.

'I'm going home today,' she said flatly.

'To Kevin?'

That startled her. 'No.' Unthinkable. At least Reith had given her that. Given her a freedom from being Kevin's little woman.

Freedom. How come it had such a sour taste?

'I'll pack and go now,' Sophie said listlessly. 'My plane doesn't leave until tonight—but I might do a bit of sightseeing on the way.' How to confess that she couldn't bear to stay here? She couldn't bear to hear Reith's truck rattle along the road and not come in.

She couldn't bear to be within a long walk of his home. . .of her heart. . .

'Oh, Sophie. . .' Moira's kindly face was a picture of distress. She guessed all, this good-hearted woman. 'I so hoped. . . You and Dr Kenrick—'

'It was an air bubble,' Sophie said brutally. She rose, sloshing her coffee in the saucer. 'You know he doesn't want anyone. How could I possibly delude myself he could ever change for me? That he could ever want me?'

She left soon after, throwing her belongings into her hire-car with savage despair.

She was going to have to pull herself together. Somehow she was going to have to build a life out of this mess.

Thank heaven for her work. At least she had her medicine. She'd go back to working in Casualty, she decided. The rush and urgency of her work there would help to drive away the ghosts of Reith Kenrick.

Who was she kidding?

Reith Kenrick would stay with her forever.

Ten minutes later Sophie pulled her car off the main gravel road. An inconspicuous sign read 'Brand Lookout'.

You have to see Brand Lookout, Moira had told her on her first day here, and Sophie had never found time. Now. . .

Now she was clear of Reith and she had hours of time before she needed to be speeding toward the airport. She could either sit in an airport lounge and stare at a book, or she could be a tourist.

Neither held very much attraction, but how long would it be before Sophie came to Australia again? Maybe never.

So be a tourist here for the last time.

It was worth the detour. Brand Lookout was a ridge overlooking the entire valley. The mountains rose above and around her in blue-purple majesty. Somewhere below was Reith's lake, and these peaks would still be reflecting their beauty long after she'd gone. Long after Reith was just a bittersweet memory.

How long she sat there she wasn't sure. Sophie left the car and walked along the ridge, then sat and swung her legs back and forth from a seat on a fallen log. The sun was hot on her face. Back home it was winter. She put her face up to the sun, drinking in its heat with a need that spoke of inner cold. She was cold to the soul.

The soft wind wafted around her, fading to nothing and then gusting in short bursts of force. Sophie's curls blew around her face. It was as if the wind was caressing—trying its darndest to heal her pain.

If she could sit here forever. . .

Crazy dream. She stood, and then stared. The wind had sprung up in a sudden gust, and hurtling toward her from the sky was a vast red bird.

It wasn't a bird. Sophie blinked twice and then realised she wasn't seeing things. It was a brilliant flame-coloured hang-glider, hurtling down toward her ridge from one of the peaks behind her.

He was badly out of control. For some reason, here in this chasm between the mountain ranges the wind was doing strange things, sweeping up and then blowing down, down. . .

He was caught in such a gust now. For one horrid moment Sophie thought he would crash into the rocks at her feet. She cringed backward; the wind relented for a split-second, the hang-glider lurched up, and then down again over the edge of the ridge where Sophie sat. It dived straight down, down into the trees below.

From somewhere beneath her, Sophie heard a crash of undergrowth and then a scream that made her cringe. The scream echoed round and round the valley and died away to nothing.

Nothing.

CHAPTER TWELVE

Sophie stood and walked slowly to the edge of the cliff. There was a handrail holding her back from the very edge, and beyond the handrail was a drop of a hundred feet or more. After that sheer drop the ground sloped outward again, to mountainside covered in thick bush.

He must be dead. . .

No. The sails of the glider would break his fall a little. The wind was driving him down, but he wasn't in free fall.

So where was he? Somewhere below?

As if in answer to her thoughts, a cry came bellowing up.

'Is someone there? Help me. . .for God's sake, help me!'

Whoever it was must have seen her as he had hurtled down out of the sky. She would have stood out where she sat on the ridge, she knew, in her white blouse and light lemon skirt.

She should go for help. There was no way she could climb down. . .

The yell from below suddenly changed in its intensity; it rose as an agonised scream. . .

Had he fallen further? Sophie wondered.

It would take half an hour to find help and bring rescuers back. If she could see. . .

Sophie lay flat on her stomach and inched forward. She wasn't good at heights at the best of times, and this was no exception. The drop made her feel sick.

It wasn't impossible, though.

Inching her nose carefully over the cliff face, Sophie saw that the drop was only sheer under the actual look out. Fifty yards from her on either side there was bush and sloped ground. The rail was placed to get the best view without the trees. If Sophie made her way through the bush at the top and then down. . .

The scream came again, sharp, agonised and cut off short. Then another.

It made the decision easy. In seconds Sophie was bashing her way through undergrowth, and then clambering down fast.

It was hard going. The drop wasn't absolutely sheer but it was close to vertical, with only enough slope to allow growth. Stunted trees fought for root space in rocky toeholds. Sophie struggled her way from one tree trunk to another, forcing her way down in the direction of the hang-glider.

She couldn't see him. She could only hear. The agonised screaming had given way to anguished sobs—a sobbing that told Sophie that, wherever he was, the man was in agony. She fought her way down fast, scratching her hands and legs, and tearing her flowing skirt in the process. Where in heaven's name was he?

And then, maybe two or three hundred yards down the cliff where the trees started growing high again, she stopped and looked up—and her breath was driven out of her body.

The man was hanging upside-down in a tree. Above him, twisted in the canopy of leaves, was what was left of the hang-glider.

How on earth was he caught? Sophie couldn't see. Was he somehow holding on by the knees? Maybe a broken arm was stopping him pulling himself up?

She stared up at the tree, measuring herself against the lowest hanging branch. She hadn't climbed a tree in twenty years, and she wasn't all that keen on trying now.

There was no choice. The sobbing started again. It cut right through her.

'I'm down below and coming up,' she called. 'Hang on.'

Of all the stupid things to say—he was hanging on for dear life.

It stopped the sobbing, though. The man froze, immobile, his body not moving an inch.

'Is. . .is someone there?' There was agony in his voice. 'Is someone—?'

'I'm coming.' Sophie cast a rueful look down at her pretty skirt, ruched it up into her knickers and started to climb. Now was hardly the time for decorum.

It took five long minutes to reach him. The man was caught thirty feet up. Sophie reached his level and stared out along the limb where he hung.

Then, as she realised why he still hung there, she sucked in her breath in dismay.

A smaller branch—almost a twig—was growing out and up from a major branch. This thick twig had pierced the man's calf. He was caught, totally helpless, the wood going right through his leg.

Her fear of heights forgotten, Sophie crawled out on the major branch with the speed of a frightened koala. The man was hanging from the injured leg. Any minute now it could tear and he'd crash to the ground.

The man could hear her coming—maybe he could see her. His view was distorted. Hanging head down as he was, it would only be a matter of time before he lost consciousness completely.

'I'm coming. . .'

It was a frightened whisper.

It wasn't quite as bad as Sophie had first thought— but bad enough. When Sophie finally reached him she realised that he'd been able to hook his uninjured leg over another small branch and take at least some of his weight.

'OK. . .I'm here.'

Sophie looped her own legs around the thicker

branch and clung for dear life. Then she reached down. 'Give me your hands.'

His hands came up and clung as hard as Sophie's legs were clinging to the branch. She was this man's lifeline, and she knew that, having proffered the lifeline, she couldn't withdraw. She either pulled him up or she'd be pulled down herself.

She pulled and clung with all her might, hauling him sideways up to her. She was pulling the man's whole weight.

His leg was still solidly pierced but the small branch causing the trouble was pliable. It should bend as he moved.

It did. The man's body lifted forward and sideways and he came up with a rush that nearly sent Sophie tumbling backward.

She held on to branch and man for dear life. The world swayed and toppled and life had never seemed so good. The alternative was falling for both of them—death.

The man screamed again as the pressure on his injured leg changed. Sophie gritted her teeth, mentally blocked her ears and clung. She had never done anything so close to physically impossible in her life before.

And finally she had him. The man's body came to rest, stable enough where he lay against her, his leg still in a crazy position, but at least he was upright and she had hold of him. His head and shoulders lay across her legs, his leg still held by the offshoot of wood.

'You're safe,' she said unsteadily. 'Just lie still and don't move your leg.'

'I. . .I won't.' It was a grinding whisper of pain. 'Who. . .who are you?'

He was a boy—no more than eighteen or nineteen, desperately young and desperately frightened. It must have been the worst kind of nightmare to have hung there alone, Sophie realised. The boy had bright red hair and freckles on ash-white skin and his lean frame trembled like a leaf in her arms.

'I'm Sophie,' Sophie told him, trying for cheerfulness in her voice and nearly succeeding. 'Sophie Lynton. And who do I have the pleasure of er. . .cuddling?'

She almost succeeded in making him smile. The pain-filled eyes creased.

'M-Mike. Mike Letherbridge.'

'Pleased to meet you, I'm sure.' Sophie's legs were aching already from the effort of holding to the branch. She had Mike's full weight straining against her but, if she let go, the offshoot through his leg would pull him down again. 'Mike, we appear to be in a bit of a predicament.'

'You. . .you could say that.'

He had courage, this lad.

'Mike, do you have friends on the mountain who'll have seen where you landed?' Sophie kept her voice deliberately even, trying not to sound anxious. If he didn't. . .

He didn't.

'N-No. I'm hang-gliding by myself.'

By himself. He had to be kidding. Surely someone knew where he was.

It seemed someone didn't.

'I came up here by myself. I know you're not supposed to—it's against the rules of the club I belong to—but I just got a new glider. I brought my glider and a motorbike to Inyabarra, left the motorbike at the bottom of the mountain where I intended to land and brought the glider up on the trailer. It would have worked really well. . .'

Except for the wind. To hang-glide in gusty conditions and alone. . .

It was hardly the time for a lecture. The boy's voice was tight and laced with pain.

'Will someone look for you tonight?' Keep the desperation out of your voice, she told herself harshly.

'N-No. University's on holidays and I told my

parents I was going away with friends. Otherwise they'd worry.'

Fancy that, Sophie thought.

So. . .so there was no one missing this boy. And there was no one missing Sophie. For how long?

Sophie's car was on the ridge. And this boy's car was higher still. Surely someone would see?

They'd assume whoever had left the car was off doing a spot of bushwalking. Camping even.

Could she somehow wedge the boy so she could go for help?

She couldn't. Sophie looked down at the wood piercing his leg. It was too thick to break. If she tried to pull it through the leg, chances were she'd tear an artery, as well as kill him from pain. And if she released him. . .well, he'd fall sideways before she was halfway back to the car. His leg would rip and he'd fall.

You couldn't even see the scarlet hang-glider from above, she thought desperately, remembering looking down and searching for a sign. It had crashed far enough through the canopy of leaves to be invisible.

So. . .

So hang on and wait.

The boy gave a soft moan and stirred in her arms. Morphine. . .she wanted morphine.

She wanted Reith.

'Reith,' she whispered over and over to herself and it was almost a prayer. 'Dear God, Reith, help me. . .

It was the longest day Sophie had ever known and afterwards she didn't know how she had found the strength to endure it.

'Leave me,' the boy groaned over and over again. 'Go and get help.'

He was in too much pain to realise what Sophie knew for sure—that if she left him he'd die. All he knew was the agony in his leg. He drifted in and out of consciousness during the day, calling for his mother.

A big, macho male, Sophie thought ruefully, with

his car and his motorbike and his hang-glider. The macho image didn't quite ring true. He had to be an indulged and beloved son, to own all this while still a student—and still a child at heart. She couldn't leave him.

She couldn't hold on forever. Her legs were cramping badly, and the whole base of her spine seemed numb. How long? How long before she fell asleep as well and fell sideways?

She was in no danger of falling asleep yet—not with the pain in her cramping legs and the ache in her arms. At least the boy wasn't heavily built—but he was heavy enough.

The day dragged on and on. Impossible situation. Impossible to stay. Impossible to go. This was crazy—to stay here. This way they could both die.

If she left he'd die almost straight away.

Reith. . .

It was a prayer—a mantra—a plea of supplication over and over again.

Useless. Reith and Moira thought she was safely on a plane to England—and even at the other end there was no one to worry when she didn't arrive.

She'd end up a skeleton dangling from a tree. . .

Oh, for heaven's sake! Sophie gave an hysterical laugh, and winced as the boy in her arms stirred. This was the way of craziness.

The sun crossed the sky with maddening slowness, shifting the shadows under the leaves. How late? Four o'clock? Five?

Then came dusk. About now she should be boarding a plane for London.

Reith. . .

The darkness was absolute. Mike was half asleep, half unconscious in her arms. Sophie was almost jealous. The pain was everywhere—in her arms, her legs, her back. . .

'Reith. . . Dear heaven, bring help. . .' She wasn't

sure who she was talking to. Anyone. Anything. She couldn't keep holding—

'Sophie!'

The call was so faint that at first she thought she was dreaming. It echoed again and again—maybe a dozen times—before she finally realised it wasn't an extension of her pathetic pleas. It was her name that was being called.

She wasn't crazy.

The pain receded. She pulled herself to sit upright, and stared up the cliff face.

She wasn't dreaming. There were lights beaming down—torches. . .

'Sophie. . .' The name echoed again out over the valley, and she knew it was Reith.

Reith. . .

His call was a cry of desperation. It rang out again and Sophie caught her breath. It held horror and hopelessness and sheer and absolute desolation.

It was the cry of a man who had lost everything he'd ever held dear in his world. It was the cry of a man bereft.

'Sophie. . .'

Sophie closed her eyes. She took a deep breath, filling her lungs with the sweet night air. Life was suddenly, immeasurably good.

'Reith!' she yelled with every ounce of power left in her exhausted body. 'I'm over here, Reith.'

Mike shifted in her arms and she clung tighter. 'Hold on, Mike. He's coming. Reith's coming. Reith!'

There was a moment's long silence and then the torchlights swung slowly toward the sound of her voice.

'Sophie?' Reith didn't sound as if he believed what was happening. He was a long way away, and his voice was dreamlike. Like Sophie, he hadn't expected respite from hopelessness.

'Reith. . .oh, Reith. . .I'm here. . .'

'Sophie!' It was a shout of joy, and then there was

the smashing of bodies through the undergrowth, swearing and crashing, and her name yelled over and over again.

And then Reith was swinging up the tree as if he had been born in the treetops, his lithe body moving fast and furiously.

She was in his arms. The weight was taken from her. Reith touched her as if he could scarcely believe she was human.

She knew how he felt. Reith. . .

Another man was there then, clambering up the tree behind Reith, and then another. She was being passed from man to man, and the pain in her legs and arms and back could finally take over.

Her whole body cramped in spasm. She cried out as she reached the ground, and Reith was swearing, and then she was drifting toward the blessedness of dark.

She couldn't let go. . .he'd fall—

'You're safe, my Sophie.' Somehow through the mist of pain she heard it. 'You're safe. We have you both. You can let go now, sweetheart. I have you safe.'

She closed her eyes and let the darkness do its worst.

She woke in her own bed.

Her own. . . It was the bed she'd stayed in for just over a week at Moira's. The bed she thought of as home more than her bed in London.

Sophie opened her eyes to the familiar pattern of light through the leaves and everything felt absolutely normal.

It was only when she moved that it didn't.

Ouch!

Her breath sucked in as the pain knifed through her. She must have made a tiny sound. The door flew open as though someone had been listening.

'Well, my love,' Moira beamed. 'Awake at last. Oh, Sophie. . .'

Sophie was enfolded in a massive embrace and Moira wept.

'We thought you were dead,' she sobbed. 'I've never been so frightened in my life. The airline rang when you didn't arrive for your ticket, and I started worrying. And I knew you were so upset, and I just thought. . .well, I just thought I might go for a drive. And I found the car by the lookout and I thought. . . oh, Sophie. . .and then. . .I thought I had to tell Dr Kenrick and I telephoned him and I think. . .I think he went a little bit crazy. . .'

And Moira burst into tears on Sophie's coverlet.

They'd thought she'd suicided.

Of course. Sophie thought of the sheer drop from the lookout—of her unhappiness, and the car abandoned at the top of the cliff.

'Oh, Moira, I'm so sorry,' she whispered.

'Sorry!' Moira's head came up at that. 'There's no need to be sorry. You saved that boy's life. They say it's a miracle you held him there as long as you did and they don't know how you did it. They had to cut the branch to get him down—and they flew him straight to Melbourne with the branch still in his leg and they've just phoned to say it's removed and there's no long-term damage and it's all down to you, my dear, and you say you're sorry?' She paused, bereft of speech, and shook her head. 'Oh, my dear. . .'

'And Reith?' It was hardly a whisper.

'He's here. He sat here all night. I tried to persuade him to go home, but he wouldn't have a bar of it. The Melbourne doctors rang to talk to him about the young hang-glider and he's in the hall taking the call now, but it was as much as I could do to get him to go to the phone. Like I said—he was a bit crazy. I don't know. . . And then, when we found you. . .'

Moira gulped and grabbed for her handkerchief. Then she paused. From the hall below, a loud tinkle announced the end of a telephone call.

'He'll come up now,' she said. 'I tried to make him go home for a shower and change—but he wouldn't. I said if you woke and saw him the way he is—his clothes ripped and scratched and bleeding—you'd faint all over again. Honest, I thought he'd rip the bush apart to get to you.' She stood, and her smile changed.

'I'll get you some breakfast,' she promised. 'Don't faint when you see Dr Kenrick. Promise?'

'I. . .I promise.'

She disappeared and Sophie hardly saw her go. Reith. . .

Sophie heard a hard, anxious demand on the stairs and then the footsteps she knew so well.

And then Reith was there. He stood in the doorway, his eyes not reassured. His face was a still, watchful mask, as though even now he was expecting to have what was precious snatched away from him.

'Reith. . .' Sophie raised herself painfully on one elbow. She knew that face. Dark and unshaven, his eyes narrowed, creased, hard with anxiety.

It wasn't a forbidding face. It was a face that expected pain.

'Reith,' she whispered and held out a hand, and he crossed the room in two long strides.

She was gathered to his heart, and her body's aches melted to nothing. Sophie flung her arms around him with a sob of love, and held him close. As close as she could be.

'My Sophie,' Reith whispered in a ragged, tearing voice. 'Oh, God. . .I thought you were dead.'

'You should know I couldn't suicide,' she whispered. 'You should know.'

'Why should I know that?' He put her away from him then, holding her at arm's length. 'You crazy, crazy girl. Why the hell should I know that? The car was there. . .' His voice broke, nightmare flooding back.

'I couldn't die,' she whispered simply. 'Because as

long as I live I have you in my heart. Even if you don't want me, I have you with me.' She touched his beloved face. 'So I intend to live for a very long time.'

The room around them faded to nothing. The whole world, it seemed, held its breath.

Then Reith swore, very softly, and pulled her against him.

'You'll have me more than in your heart, my precious Sophie,' he growled, his voice husky with emotion. 'I didn't know one crazy woman could tear me in two. I didn't know it was too late to send you away. The damage was done. To lose you was like losing life itself—worse. From here on, my love, my life, you'll have me in your life forever. If you'll have me.'

Sophie's eyes widened. That he could say that to her. . . If you'll have me. . .

'I'll have you, my Reith,' she whispered. 'With all my heart.'

CHAPTER THIRTEEN

SOPHIE woke with the dawn.

The warm breeze was blowing gently through the half-open flap of the tent. It caressed Sophie's body—the small amount of naked skin that wasn't already being caressed.

Reith had found thick feather-down bed-rolls for his bride. They billowed round the couple now in a pile of feathery softness. Satin sheets were there to cover them and there were light wool blankets to keep any chill at bay.

The sheets and blankets hadn't been needed. Their wedding night had been all Sophie had dreamed it could be, and Sophie needed no other cover than her beloved Reith.

He slept on now beside her, his harsh face easing its look of solitude in sleep.

There was no more solitude for Reith.

Sophie lay entwined in his arms, letting her mind drift over the previous day. Her wedding day.

Moira had hostessed their wedding, proudly organising the marriage of her beloved Sophie. She bullied Sophie into traditional white, aided by Gilda from Gilda's Gourmet Goodies—who also turned out to be Gilda, seamstress extraordinaire. Sophie had been married in a mist of white tulle and satin, with Mandy as flower-girl accompanying the bride in a swirling flounce of pink pride.

Half the valley had been there, and a few others. Mike Letherbridge, her rescued hang-glider, had been there on crutches and minus anything remotely macho male. Mary and Ted had been glowing over their flower-girl daughter. Margaret Lee had arrived extol-

ling the virtues of a sugar-free diet. Even Christabelle
and Elvira Pilkington had been there, free of chickenpox and content, for once, to let Sophie be the centre
of attention.

Though she hadn't been the centre of attention,
Sophie thought blissfully.

Reith had. How could he not have been in her eyes,
impossibly handsome in his black dinner suit, with one
red rose in his lapel proudly declaring his love?

He hadn't needed the rose. His love had been there
for all to see, holding Sophie in thrall. The beautiful
ceremony washed over her in a mist of happiness and
she could remember little. All she saw was her Reith.

Sophie remembered the car, though. When it was
time to drive away Sophie had looked for Reith's awful
truck and found it gone—a luxurious, four-wheel-drive
sedan in its place.

'You can't take a twenty-year-old truck on a luxury
honeymoon,' Reith had teased, refusing to reveal his
plans. 'Nothing but the best for my Sophie—from this
day forth.'

She would have gone anywhere with him, in a wheel-
barrow if necessary, but when she had been where he
had taken her Sophie's heart had cried out with delight.

Her lake and her mountains. The setting for *Bush
Bride*.

'I've organised a locum for a month and in two days
we'll fly to London to face your mother,' Reith had
told her. 'Maybe after that we'll go to Italy. . .maybe
luxurious hotels then, my love. But for these two
days I thought we could stay here. This is where we
belong, my Sophie.' And then his eyes creased in sudden doubt. 'I'm not wrong, am I, my love?' he asked
anxiously, gathering her bridal beauty close. 'You did
say you loved it here—but, if you want, we can go
somewhere else.'

Sophie gazed down at their camp site through a mist
of tears. The lake was reflecting its crimson splendour.

The sun was setting on her first day of married life and she couldn't think of anything more perfect.

'But this is my place, my Reith,' she whispered and held him close. 'I'm your bush bride. Now and forever. . .'

They were the last words she had spoken for a long, long time.

The recollections faded. Sophie stirred, stretching her body languorously in the warmth. Reith was so close. . .he was part of her, and she knew that tomorrow and tomorrow and tomorrow he would always be here.

She could ask for no more.

Then she stiffened. From outside the tent came a massive roar—a roar she had heard only once before.

Reith's eyes opened and his arms tightened around her.

'Afraid, my Sophie?' He had felt her stiffen.

'It's. . .I know it's only a koala.'

Reith grinned, sat up and flung the tent flap wide. There on the grass before them sat a small grey koala.

A very familiar koala. . .

Sophie stared at the scar running down from his eye. She looked at the patch of fur missing from his leg in absolute amazement. It couldn't be. Could it?

'The very same,' Reith smiled, shaking his head in disbelief. 'You get around, fella.'

The koala glared.

'Look, I know it was you who brought us together, and I'm sorry to be unsocial, mate,' Reith grinned, 'but you can go practise your mating calls somewhere else. This lady's taken.'

Reith closed the tent flap, fastening it tight. The koala was left staring in indignation. Then Reith turned to Sophie. His dark eyes gleamed wicked intention down at his bride.

'Well, my love?'

'W-well?' Her heart was pounding at the look of

him. Her naked Reith. . . Her husband. . .

'Do you need the odd growl to get you in the mating mood, my heart?'

Sophie smiled up at him. Her hands reached out to hold him—to pull him down to her. His heart. . .

'No growls,' she whispered, and her voice was husky with love and desire. 'My Reith, I've mated with you for the rest of my life.'

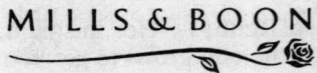

MILLS & BOON

Back by Popular Demand

BETTY NEELS

A collector's edition of forty favourite titles from one of the world's best-loved romance authors.

Mills & Boon are proud to bring back these sought after titles, now reissued in beautifully matching volumes and presented together in one cherished collection.

Don't miss these unforgettable titles, coming next month:

Title #1 THE DOUBTFUL MARRIAGE
Title #2 A GEM OF A GIRL

Available wherever
Mills & Boon books are sold

MILLS & BOON

Romancing a royal was easy, marriage another affair!

If you love Hello! magazine then you'll love our brand new three part series **Royal Affair** by popular author Stephanie Howard.

In each book you can read about the glamorous and of course romantic lives of each of the royal siblings in the San Rinaldo dukedom—the heir to the dukedom, his sister and their playboy brother.

Don't miss:

The Colorado Countess in May '96
The Lady's Man in June '96
The Duke's Wife in July '96

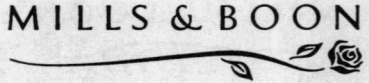

MILLS & BOON

MEDICAL ROMANCE

LOVE ON CALL

The books for enjoyment this month are:

BUSH DOCTOR'S BRIDE	Marion Lennox
FORGOTTEN PAIN	Josie Metcalfe
COUNTRY DOCTORS	Gill Sanderson
COURTING DR GROVES	Meredith Webber

Treats in store!

Watch next month for the following absorbing stories:

TENDER TOUCH	Caroline Anderson
LOVED AND LOST	Margaret Barker
THE SURGEON'S DECISION	Rebecca Lang
AN OLD-FASHIONED PRACTICE	Carol Wood

Available from W.H. Smith, John Menzies, Volume One,
Forbuoys, Martins, Woolworths, Tesco, Asda, Safeway and
other paperback stockists.

Readers in South Africa - write to:
IBS, Private Bag X3010, Randburg 2125.

Name that Song

How would you like to win a year's supply of simply irresistible romances? Well, you can and they're free! Simply solve the puzzle below and send your completed entry to us by 31st October 1996. The first five correct entries picked after the closing date will each win a years supply of Temptation novels (four books every month—worth over £100).

Please turn over for details of how to enter 🖙

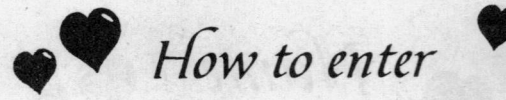 *How to enter*

To solve our puzzle…first circle eight well known girls names hidden in the grid. Then unscramble the remaining letters to reveal the title of a well-known song (five words).

When you have written the song title in the space provided below, don't forget to fill in your name and address, pop this page into an envelope (you don't need a stamp) and post it today! Hurry—competition ends 31st October 1996.

**Mills & Boon Song Puzzle
FREEPOST
Croydon
Surrey
CR9 3WZ**

Song Title: _____

Are you a Reader Service Subscriber?   Yes ❏   No ❏

Ms/Mrs/Miss/Mr _____

Address _____

_____

_____ Postcode _____

One application per household.

You may be mailed with other offers from other reputable companies as a result of this application. If you would prefer not to receive such offers, please tick box. ❏

C396
D